How to Manage Conflict

3rd Edition

Turn All Conflicts into Win-Win Outcomes

by Peg Pickering

Career Press
Franklin Lakes, NJ

CAREER
PRESS

Career Press endorses nonsexist language. In an effort to make this handbook clear, consistent, and easy to read, we have used "he" throughout the odd-numbered chapters, and "she" throughout the even-numbered chapters. The copy is not intended to be sexist.

HOW TO MANAGE CONFLICT, 3RD EDITION
Cover design by Barry Littmann
Printed in the U.S.A. by Book-mart Press

To order this title, please call toll-free 1-800-CAREER-1 (NJ and Canada: 201-848-0310) to order using VISA or MasterCard, or for further information on books from Career Press.

The Career Press, Inc., 3 Tice Road, PO Box 687,
Franklin Lakes, NJ 07417

Library of Congress Cataloging-in-Publication Data

Pickering, Peg
    How to manage conflict : turn all conflicts into win-win outcomes /
by Peg Pickering.--3rd ed.
        p. cm.
    Includes index.
    ISBN 1-56414-440-2 (paper)
    1. Conflict management. I. Title.

HM1126.953 2000
303.6'9--dc21   99-051920

Table of Contents

INTRODUCTION

As the pace of life and business continues to accelerate, the opportunities for conflicts multiply. Yet, the ability to work well with others is the single greatest determinant of success in the 21st century. Therefore, learning to disarm and defuse confrontational situations and people is essential. One cannot work effectively with others with clenched fists.

Managing conflict effectively requires developing competency in five areas:

1. Understand the critical ingredients for collaborative thinking.

2. Align responsibilities to the needs of others.

3. Build into daily interactions the practices necessary for support.

4. Have conflict resolution skills and negotiation skills to resolve various types of challenges.

5. Begin developing personal tools and systems for dealing with tensions and pressures.

One's ability to build these competencies hinges on four success factors:

- Personal responsibility for one's own learning and skill development.

- Flexibility of style.

- Ability to listen and provide feedback on what is heard.

- A positive attitude toward change.

Read this handbook carefully and refer to it in the future. Be sure to complete each set of Reflections to immediately put these critical concepts and principles to work in your life.

1 FUNDAMENTALS OF CONFLICT

Understanding conflict – its causes and effects – is fundamental to personal and professional success. Your ability to deal effectively with people, to elicit cooperation even in trying situations, has never been more important than it is today. When you have completed this chapter, you'll be able to more clearly define conflict, identify both its positive and negative effects, and dispel the five most common misconceptions about it.

What Is Conflict and Why Do We Have So Much of It?

Daniel Webster defines conflict as:

1. competitive or opposing action of incompatibles

2. antagonistic state or action (as of divergent ideas, interests or persons)

3. struggle resulting from incompatible needs, drives, wishes or demands

4. hostile encounter

In essence, conflict exists when two or more competing responses or courses of action to a single event are considered. Conflict does not necessarily imply hostility, although hostility can certainly become part of the situation.

Conflict is merely the existence of competing or incompatible options.

That's simple. Maybe too simple. Conflict in today's fast-paced, contentious society is inevitable and rampant. Everywhere you turn, there's "the existence of competing or incompatible options."

- Your perfume allergy places you in conflict with many individuals daily.

- You struggle with the same idiots on the freeway going to and from work each day.

- Your career and family create constant time and commitment conflicts.

- A neighbor is threatening to sue you over some trivial disagreement.

- There are so many things you want to accomplish that you're at a loss where to start.

- Your values and ethics cause perpetual internal re-examination as you face situational ethics throughout society.

- Your children have decided they know everything and you know nothing.

- Some days you fear your boss agrees with your children!

Sound all too familiar? Unfortunately, there's more bad news. The potential for conflict will continue to grow exponentially as the pace of our society continues to accelerate. With explosive technological advances comes an avalanche of change. Change brings uncertainty, fear, and discomfort, which is fertile ground for conflict. As a result, conflict resolution skills that were an advantage in the late 20th century are *essential* for mere survival in the 21st.

There is good news, however. Contrary to popular belief, conflict is not always a bad thing. In fact, properly handled conflict can provide numerous benefits to both the individuals involved and their organizations.

Potential Positive Effects of Conflict

- Increased motivation

- Enhanced problem/solution identification

- Group cohesiveness

- Reality adjustment

- Increased knowledge/skill

- Enhanced creativity

- Contribution to goal attainment

- Incentive for growth

These benefits cannot be realized, however, if the conflict is ignored or poorly handled. In such instances, conflict becomes detrimental or even destructive.

Potential Negative Effects of Conflict

- Decreased productivity

- Erosion of trust

- Coalition formation with polarized positions

- Secrecy and reduced information flow

- Morale problems

- Consumption of mass amounts of time

- Decision-making paralysis

Obviously, learning to handle conflict effectively is critical. Before immersing yourself in conflict management techniques, five common misconceptions about conflict need to be addressed.

Common Misconceptions About Conflict

1. Conflict, if left alone, will take care of itself.

2. Confronting an issue or person is always unpleasant.

3. The presence of conflict in an organization is a sign of a poor manager.

4. Conflict among staff is a sign of low concern for the organization.

5. Anger is always negative and destructive.

Misconception #1: Conflict, if left alone, will take care of itself.

Wouldn't that be nice! Typically, the longer a conflict is ignored, the more difficult it becomes. It escalates to higher and higher levels of intensity until it becomes so unbearable that it can no longer be ignored.

Unfortunately, a conflict will dissipate by itself on occasion. Why, you ask, is that unfortunate? If you've ever had a conflict disappear on its own accord, you increase your tendency to hold back, refrain from facing the issues and avoid dealing with the next conflict in the hope that it, too, will magically dissipate. And while you're waiting, the conflict is gaining a life of its own, rising like bread dough, and becoming more and more unmanageable.

Misconception #2: Confronting an issue or a person is always unpleasant.

Many people would almost rather be shot than have a confrontation! Just the word makes the hair on the back of the neck stand up. But confronting something does not have to involve a nasty exchange. To confront simply means:

1. To face, especially in challenge

2. To oppose

3. To cause to meet

4. To bring face to face

Confronting an issue or person simply means putting the items in question on the table to be addressed. Without this examination, the conflict cannot be successfully resolved. But once the problem(s) have been properly identified and well-defined, they are already half-solved.

Keep in mind: Behavior not confronted will not change. If someone is doing something or behaving in a way that is unacceptable to you, you must bring it to their attention. You must confront the issue. Specific techniques to do so can be found in Chapter 6.

Misconception #3: The presence of conflict in an organization is a sign of a poor manager.

The mere existence of conflict means nothing. It in no way reflects on a manager's ability. How well the manager deals with conflict when it arises and how he anticipates potential future problems are the true measures of the strength of his management skills.

Willie Shoemaker, the jockey who rode the winning Triple Crown horse in the 1960s, was an extraordinary jockey in part because of his excellent control. The horse never felt his hand on the rein unless it was needed. A good manager has this "soft set of hands" during conflict.

Misconception #4: Conflict among staff is a sign of low concern for the organization.

Why would people invest enormous amounts of time and emotional energy on things of no consequence to them? People tend to be emotionally involved in things they care about. Therefore, conflict can be a sign of genuine concern. Conflict can help clarify emotions and serves to identify underlying values.

Misconception #5: Anger is always negative and destructive.

When aired at lower stages of conflict, anger can be cathartic, helping the parties more clearly identify the issues and values involved. At higher levels of conflict, however, explosive anger can have the opposite effect.

Anger itself is neither positive nor negative. How we choose to utilize that anger, however, is vital to our success in managing conflict. How well we control that anger and our overall stress level will dramatically impact our ability to effectively handle life's conflicts.

Below are 25 situations in which conflict and anger are likely to arise. Think carefully about each situation, rate on a scale of 1 - 5 the volatility of your typical reaction, and circle your response. (1 indicates a relatively calm reaction and 5 indicates a major eruption.)

1. As you're about to leave home for an important appointment, you spill coffee on your clothing.
   1 2 3 4 5

2. A car pulls out in front of you, causing you to slam on your brakes, and the other driver gestures at you as if you'd done something wrong.
   1 2 3 4 5

3. You miss a deadline at work because information to be supplied by someone else arrives late.
   1 2 3 4 5

4. A waiter or waitress gets your order all wrong, and you're served a meal you don't want.
   1 2 3 4 5

5. Friends arrive at your door unexpectedly, assuming that you're ready to entertain them.
   1 2 3 4 5

6. You must wait an extremely long time at a medical or dental office.
   1 2 3 4 5

7. You drop a gallon of milk, spilling it all over the floor.
   1 2 3 4 5

8. You're driving behind a car going ten miles under the legal speed limit, and there is no way you can pass.
   1 2 3 4 5

9. You get a ticket for parking illegally.
   1 2 3 4 5

10. Someone makes fun of your new haircut.
    1 2 3 4 5

Reflections
Reflections

11. At work, a recent effort is criticized by your boss in front of several of your colleagues.
    1   2   3   4   5

12. At the last minute, a friend cancels out of plans you'd made for the evening.
    1   2   3   4   5

13. Someone takes credit for work you did.
    1   2   3   4   5

14. You discover that someone is gossiping about you.
    1   2   3   4   5

15. Someone to whom you're speaking doesn't even pretend to be listening to you.
    1   2   3   4   5

16. A friend borrows something of yours — car, book, clothing, etc. — and returns it damaged and makes no mention of its condition.
    1   2   3   4   5

17. Your judgment or intelligence is called into question.
    1   2   3   4   5

18. A pen breaks in the pocket of your favorite suit.
    1   2   3   4   5

19. An expensive item of clothing returns from the cleaners with a large stain on it.
    1   2   3   4   5

20. Someone at work goes through your desk drawers without your permission.
    1   2   3   4   5

21. At the very last minute, you are asked to make a presentation at work on a subject with which you are mostly unfamiliar.
    1   2   3   4   5

Reflections

22. Your spouse or partner makes a major purchase without consulting you.
    1   2   3   4   5

23. Friends bring their toddler to your home and sit silently as the child wreaks havoc on your belongings.
    1   2   3   4   5

24. Despite your certainty, you are unable to convince your bank that they have made an error adversely affecting your balance.
    1   2   3   4   5

25. A friend tells someone else personal information you've revealed in confidence.
    1   2   3   4   5

Add the numbers you've circled. If your total score is:

25 - 50:   While there is probably always room for improvement, you remain admirably calm in the face of potentially vexing situations. You have learned there are other options besides anger as reactions to change and sudden or unpleasant developments.

51 - 100:   Your ability to contain conflict and anger at generally manageable and non-destructive levels still needs work. You opt for anger more often than you should.

101-125:   You literally are in the process of killing yourself. Volcanic reactions like yours to life's difficult situations do harm to your health. It is probable that you have jeopardized or completely lost some friendships and/or working relationships. Improving your skills is essential to survival.

Reflections

2 TYPES OF CONFLICT

Categorizing conflicts, their causes, and the typical reactions to them can be a complex undertaking. When you've completed this chapter, you'll have a firm understanding of internal, interpersonal, intra- and inter-group conflicts as well as the differences between substantive, personality, and communication-based conflicts. Additionally, you'll be able to identify the psychological needs at the base of much conflict as well as the four categories of reactions.

Internal Conflict

Internal conflict is a disturbance that which rages within oneself. It involves emotional dissonance for an individual when expertise, interest, goals, or values are stretched to meet certain tasks or expectations beyond the comfort level or when these items are in direct conflict with each other. Internal conflict reflects the gap between what you say you want and what you do about it. It hampers daily life and can immobilize some people.

At the mildest levels of internal conflict, you'll have headaches and possibly backaches. Stress management techniques are a critical antidote for this type of conflict. When we reach the "burnout" levels of stress, we are at stage two of internal conflict. The destructive nature of suicidal thoughts are an example of stage three.

11

How an individual copes with internal conflict will determine whether interpersonal conflict can be effectively addressed. Conflict can't be managed externally until you have control of yourself internally!

Here are self-assessment questions to help you determine whether internal conflict is a current issue for you.

- Are there people you avoid? Avoidance is a coping mechanism and usually allows for low levels of stress and conflict.

- Do you find yourself looking for some release from the day-to-day pressures of work? One school of thought teaches that we can vent our feelings and emotions by redirecting the energy into other activities. This does work for some. The important point is to be aware of our need to vent since it's another sign of internal conflict.

- Do you find it nearly impossible to get out of a problem-solving mode, even after you've left the office? If you care about an issue, you are more likely to experience stress over its lack of resolution. Conflict is one barometer of our concern. An inability to "put things aside" indicates an internal seething common to those struggling with internal conflict.

- Are you more short-tempered than you used to be or than you'd like to be?

- Do you feel you have few choices in your life? That there is an abundance of things you "have to do"?

- Do you find yourself complaining more and more frequently?

- Do you have sudden bursts of energy and start multiple projects only to run out of steam and abandon them unfinished?

- Do you find yourself coming up with "perfectly good reasons" not to change?

Don't despair if you answered yes to most or even all of the questions above. Most people do. Internal conflict can be an alerting mechanism that shows you where energy is being drained away and where you need to focus your personal management skills.

Interpersonal Conflict

Interpersonal conflict is that which exists between individuals. Every human being has four basic psychological needs which, when violated, will automatically spark a conflict: the need to be valued and treated as an individual, to be in control, to have strong self-esteem, and to be consistent.

- The need to be valued and treated as an individual. We all want to have others recognize our worth and to value us and our contribution. That is why recognition is the best motivator for people. We love to be told what we've done right and to be given credit for our ideas. When we feel unappreciated, taken for granted, or taken advantage of, our need to be valued has been violated, triggering our fear/anger response.

- The need to be in control. Being in control is an issue for everyone ... more for some than others. Most excessively controlling people are really very insecure. The more secure you feel within yourself, the less need you have to control others. Keep this in mind the next time you must deal with a very controlling individual.

- The need for self-esteem. Strong self-esteem lays a solid foundation for dealing appropriately with all types of situations. It is the key to our ability to respond rather than react.
Responding to a problem indicates a positive, controlled, solution-oriented approach.
Reacting is a negative, and frequently inappropriate, emotional, knee-jerk answer. (For example, the patient is responding to treatment vs. reacting to a medication.)

- The need to be consistent. Once you've dug in your heels and taken a hard stand on an issue, it's difficult to reverse yourself and admit you are wrong. The need to be consistent coupled with the need to be right makes saving face an important factor in most conflicts.

When these needs are violated, human beings react in one of four ways: we retaliate, dominate, isolate, or cooperate.

Retaliate: "I don't get mad, I get even." In many instances retaliation feels like a good option. The momentary satisfaction of getting back at the other party is tempting (like the airline attendant who routed the bags of an obnoxious Cleveland-bound passenger to Tokyo instead!) But *retaliation is always a mistake*. That fleeting moment of victory always precipitates even greater conflicts down the road. What goes around, comes around.

Dominate: "My way or else!" Bullying behavior and running roughshod over the other party are common responses for some. People with short tempers and strong opinions may fall into the domination mode automatically if they are not extremely careful. While there are times when this approach is appropriate (immediate safety and security issues), it is typically very hard on the long-term relationship and will invariably spark additional problems later.

Isolate: Sometimes simply accepting or ignoring the situation without response is a good idea. Just be sure you have truly accepted it as opposed to suppressing it. If you can *accept it and let it go*, great. If, however, it continues to bother you, to fester inside, to build upon other issues you've ignored, it's a time bomb just waiting to explode. At some point, your charming, easy-going personality will turn ugly for little or no apparent reason as the lid blows off the pressure keg. Your desire to avoid confronting a small issue up front has turned it into a much larger, much less easily managed situation.

Cooperate: The last and preferred option is to confront the issue immediately. Many people recoil at the concept of confrontation and think it, by definition, must be a loud, unpleasant experience. To confront an issue simply means to address it and put it on the table for discussion.

As previously stated, *behavior not confronted will not change*. If someone is doing something you find troublesome, you must address it if you want it to change. Amazingly, many people engaging in problematic behavior have no idea they're doing anything disturbing. Almost half of them will change that behavior as soon as its bothersome nature is brought to their attention. Half! But if you fail to confront the problem, they are not even aware of the need for a change and your cause is lost because of your own inaction. Each individual must take personal responsibility for raising issues of importance to him and communicate concerns clearly.

Types of Interpersonal Conflict

Individuals in conflict typically believe they know the cause of the conflict, but they are frequently wrong. By the time a conflict reaches a level where people are willing to deal with it, the real conflict is actually an accumulation of half-remembered and relatively minor issues. Many times, people are not even sure what the basis of the conflict is.

- Is it a substantive conflict? Issue based? A conflict about decisions ideas, directions, actions?

- Is it a personalized conflict? Personality based? Fueled by emotion? Does it question motives and character?

- Is it simply a problem of communication?

Group Dynamics of Conflict

Intragroup conflict is that which exists between individuals within a particular group (team, department, company, etc.) while intergroup involves more than one group (multiple teams, departments, organizations, etc.). The group aspect of these conflicts further complicates them. Not only must individuals deal with their internal issues and with each other as individuals, they must cope with the overall interaction of all the players. Frequently, group conflicts take on a life of their own and problems are magnified by politics, rumor, and innuendo. This multiplication of issues creates additional layers of complexity to each conflict.

Intergroup conflict is the most complex and most serious to the organization. Any time conflict escalates and spreads among groups, the gossip and rumor mill create havoc and damage you and your business.

It is best to address conflict when it involves only the smallest segment of people. An excellent first step is to classify the event and identify what it is doing to you personally, who else is involved and whether the conflict has spread from a localized, tightly focused situation to a broader-based conflict involving more people.

You can always assume that the increase in people brings generalized problems that are less clearly defined and much more likely to require multiple solutions. The likelihood of destruction and harm to others increases greatly once multiple personalities become involved.

Once you have assessed the conflict, a conflict management/resolution strategy can be selected. These strategies are discussed in detail in Chapters 4 and 5.

• How much internal conflict do you have in your life? (Review the questions in the Internal Conflict section of this chapter.) What's your stress level? List three things you can do to immediately move toward greater inner peace.

• Which of the four psychological needs are most frequently triggered in you? What can you do to lower that threshold?

• Of the four reaction styles: retaliate, dominate, isolate or cooperate which is your standard response? Ask three other people who know you well to see whether your perception matches theirs. How will you become more likely to cooperate rather than the behaviors listed as other choices?

Reflections

Read each statement and circle the response that most reflects your belief.

Part I. When my stress level is minimal and manageable:

1. I have no doubts about what I want from life and work.

   Usually   Sometimes   Always   Never

2. I _____ most people.

   Like   Trust   Evaluate   Dislike

3. What I usually do with my opinions:

   Voice them to others   Keep them to myself

4. I live up to my promises:

   Because I want to   Because I need to

   If I have to   When I can

5. I describe problems as:

   Opportunities   Something to make the best of
   Caused by stupid mistakes   Normal way of life

6. My goals are:

   Well chosen   Somewhat realistic
   Admirable   Same as always

7. On a good day I:

   Treat people and tasks equally
   Concentrate on keeping people happy
   Concentrate on getting job done
   Concentrate on getting through the day

Reflections

Read each statement and circle the response that most reflects your belief.

Part II. When my stress level is rising:

1. I am sincere and considerate of others:

   Most of the time   Sometimes
   Even when they don't   When I can deserve it

2. My decisions are made:

   Easily   Carefully   Quickly   Alone

3. Mistakes add to my:

   Growth   Embarrassment   Frustration   Despair

4. When I'm really stressed I am:

   Hopeful   Careful   Forceful   Depressed

5. When I'm really stressed I am:

   Confident   Still a nice person
   As patient as I can be   Not my usual self

6. My sense of purpose and direction is:

   Clear   Weak   Right   Absent

7. On a bad day I am:

   My own best friend   My own biggest obstacle
   The only one I can count on   No good to anybody

Reflections

3 IDENTIFYING CONFLICT STAGES

Effective conflict management results when you develop and implement a deliberate conflict strategy. The intensity of the conflict determines which strategies will be the most effective. Different levels of conflict involve varying degrees of emotional involvement and intensity.

As conflict escalates, each individual's concern for self increases along with the desire to win. Saving face takes on increased importance at higher levels of conflict. Even normally mild-mannered individuals can become hostile and hurtful as conflict escalates.

If conflict is identified early and deliberate steps are taken to modify events and manage the emotions, almost any conflict can become a source of opportunity. Left unchecked, conflict is potentially dangerous to all involved.

When you've completed this chapter, you'll be able to identify the stages of conflict, characteristics of each, and methods for effectively dealing with conflict at each level. Additionally, you'll be able to assess your own situation(s).

Three Stages of Conflict

Stage One: Everyday Concerns and Disputes. The least threatening of conflicts, stage one conflicts can best be addressed with coping strategies.

Stage Two: More Significant Challenges. With their longer-term consequences and higher emotional involvement, managing stage two conflicts requires more training and specific management skills.

Stage Three: Overt Battles. Even nice people can become harmful to others during stage three conflict when volatile emotions are raging and the desire to win is surpassed by the desire to punish.

Conflict moves between stages but not necessarily in a linear pattern. A stage one conflict on Monday morning, left unattended, can escalate to stage three by the end of the day. Conversely, high levels of conflict may dissipate with time, quite unexpectedly. Given this fickle nature of conflict, a complete understanding of the characteristics and strategies appropriate for each stage is needed.

Characteristics of Stage One Conflict — Everyday Concerns and Disputes

Stage one conflict is real, although low in intensity. This stage is characterized by day-to-day irritations. Most individuals employ coping strategies unconsciously, and these coping skills are an excellent tool for these conflicts. But coping strategies, such as tolerating the actions of co-workers, are most effective when they are deliberate rather than unconscious. Care must be taken so these irritations do not turn into bigger problems.

The critical variable here is people. Different personalities, coping mechanisms, and ever-changing life events make it impossible to predict when an individual has had enough. What was tolerable yesterday may become an issue tomorrow. There's no way to truly know which "straw will break the camel's back."

When people work together, differences exist in goals, values, and individual needs. At stage one, parties feel discomfort and possibly anger but are quick to pass off these emotions. Individuals are usually willing to work toward a solution, often with a sense of optimism that things can be worked out.

This optimism might be detected as a "no big deal" attitude. Facts and opinions are shared openly with one another once the problem has surfaced. Communication is usually clear, specific, and solution oriented — focused on the issues, not the personalities.

The easiest way to discern whether you are in a stage one conflict or a more intense level is to observe participants' ability to separate people from the problem. Brainstorming and creative problem-solving work well at stage one because participants are willing to discuss problems rather than personalities.

Listening and participation are essential at this level. As a conflict manager, initiate joint listening and exploration ventures with an emphasis on teamwork and shared responsibility. This strategy focuses all the participants in a common direction and allows everyone to contribute.

Coping Strategies for Stage One Conflict

Avoidance is one effective coping strategy for stage one conflicts. The deliberate coping strategy of avoidance happens when you determine there is neither time nor motivation to alter the idiosyncrasies of another. You pass off minor things rather than deal with them. You keep silent on an issue rather than spark a spirited discussion with your boss. If your contact with the person is minimal, the chances are good that you have managed the irritation appropriately. At this stage, a "live and let live" attitude works well.

But beware. Too many irritations can create undercurrents that, if not addressed, will complicate future issues. Remember your grade school playground when teams were picked and friends paired off? Instantly, a coping strategy was initiated by those doing the choosing and those chosen last. The games went on, but feelings of alienation were sometimes generated and carried for months, even years, to come. Similar feelings are produced during daily contacts with other people.

Obliging is a slightly stronger form of avoidance, where an individual gives in to another. Obliging involves one's desire to fit in and belong. This desire is usually strong and overrides lower levels of conflict. This strategy uses a give-in attitude so things can keep moving. Deliberate obliging can be beneficial to team effort, but there is no way to predict how long an individual will oblige.

Additional stage one conflict strategies might include:

- Initiating a process that examines both sides. Can a framework be built that encourages understanding of one another?

- Asking if the reaction is proportional to the situation. Is either party carrying residual emotions from another event? Is this event isolated or do the feelings reflect previous disagreements?

- Identifying points of agreement and working from these points first; then identifying points of disagreement. Is it possible to leap the hurdle of conflict by seeing the whole picture?

Characteristics of Stage Two Conflict — More Significant Challenges

Conflict takes on the element of competition at stage two, typified by a win-lose attitude. Losses seem greater at this stage because people are more personally invested in the problems. Self-interest and saving face becomes very important. A "cover yourself" attitude can also be observed. At stage two people keep track of verbal victories and record mistakes, witnesses take sides, and an imaginary debate develops with scores being tallied. Alliances and cliques begin to form. As a result, the level of commitment required to work through stage two conflict is significantly higher than that required at stage one.

Notice the words people select to describe a conflict or disagreement. In a stage two conflict, the language is less specific; people talk in generalizations. You'll hear references to the phantom "they" and comments like "everyone believes." Words of exaggeration like "always" and "never" increase in frequency during stage two conflict.

Because the conflict is more complex at stage two, problems can no longer be managed with coping strategies. At this stage, the people are the problem. A discussion of the issues often proves futile as parties continually drift into personality concerns. In fact, you notice resistance when attempts are made to address the issues directly.

It's important to note that the atmosphere is not necessarily hostile at stage two; but it is very cautious! Put-downs, sarcasm, and innuendoes are survival tactics used during stage two conflict. The coping strategies such as avoidance and obliging that worked so well at stage one are ineffective at stage two. A "wait-and-see" attitude degenerates into a "you prove yourself to me" attitude at stage two. Competing parties are less likely to provide accurate facts to one another because the trust level has declined.

To manage conflict effectively at stage two, you must implement a people management strategy.

Management Strategies to Handle Stage Two Conflict

- Create a safe atmosphere. Provide an environment where everyone is secure.

  — Make the setting informal

  — Establish neutral turf

  — Have an agenda

  — Be in control

  — Set the tone

  — Be slightly vulnerable

- Be hard on the facts, soft on the people. Take an extended amount of time to get every detail. Clarify generalizations. Who are "they"? Is "always" an accurate statement? Question whether any fact was missed.

- Do the initial work as a team, sharing in the

responsibility for finding an alternative everyone can live with. Stress the necessity of equal
responsibility.

- Look for middle ground but do not suggest
  compromise. Compromise implies giving up
  cherished points. Instead, creatively look for
  the middle ground by focusing on points of
  agreement.

- Allow time to pull competing parties toward
  acceptable ground without forcing issues or
  concessions.

- Competing parties should be seated next to
  each other rather than across a table. A round
  table also works well.

Stage two conflict left unchecked will delude thinking
and magnify the problems. Conflicting parties see themselves as more benevolent and others as more evil than is
actually the case. When you notice comments that focus on
either/or or black and white thinking, conflict has escalated
into stage three.

Characteristics of Stage Three Conflict —
Overt Battles

At stage three, the objective shifts from wanting to win
toward wanting to hurt. The motivation is to get rid of the
other party. Changing the situation and problem-solving are
no longer satisfactory for those locked into stage three conflict. Being right and punishing those who are wrong
becomes the consuming motivation.

Individuals choose sides on the issues that matter and insiders and outsiders are identified by the competing parties. "What's good for me" and "What's good for the organization" become synonymous in the minds of individuals holding a position in a stage three conflict.

Leaders emerge from the group and act as spokespersons. Positions are polarized; small factions evolve and group cohesiveness is more important than organizational unity. The merits of an argument and the strength with which positions are held are greatly exaggerated at this stage. A loss of perspective is quite likely on the part of all participants.

Logic and reason are not effective in dissuading others at this stage. Because everyone will not hold stage three intensity in the conflict, identify those individuals who are at the lower stages of conflict and begin redirecting these individuals, providing an alternative source for their energy.

Clear corporate goals and a sense of direction will be necessary for individuals to walk away from stage three conflict as winners. The good conflict manager delegates tasks to people and redirects events, encouraging the skills of everyone. This is not the time to cover up the event, but it need not be the all-consuming issue individuals have made it out to be.

Intervention Strategies for Stage Three Conflict

When conflict escalates to stage three, the best strategy you can employ is to minimize the losses and prepare to refocus those who remain. What do you do with the losers? Possible replacement or outplacement can be tried. A cooling off period for the losers might also be initiated once a decision is made. It is vital that you have a complete grasp of the negotiation/arbitration process, or you may find you have nothing left to manage.

One tactic you should consider once you observe stage three attitudes is the initiation of an intervention team that is neutral to the groups in conflict. For example, members from a disinterested department could be formed to address the concerns and issues of each party. The role of such an intervention team could take the form of negotiation, mediation, or arbitration.

- Negotiation: Requires parties to sit across from one another and work through the conflict in the presence of an outside agent. This process, once begun, can produce solutions to the problem but is not likely to produce harmony. At stage three, parties have decided that someone must go.

- Mediation: Both sides present their case to the intervention team and the team facilitates discussion and encourages movement toward a mutually acceptable solution. Usually, the opposing parties remain responsible for finding common ground and solutions in mediation.

- Arbitration: Each side presents its best case; the intervention team chooses one side over the other. There is obviously a great deal to be lost by both sides once this tactic is used but it can bring an end to high level conflict. Arbitration, especially binding arbitration, demands enforcement. All parties must follow and accept the conclusions of the intervention team.

The members of an intervention team must be perceived as totally impartial, able to provide a fair hearing for everyone. This intervention team will be required to sift through many emotions in search of facts and must also provide clear-cut direction at the conclusion of the fact-finding process.

Individuals locked into a stage three conflict will likely prolong the conflict, consumed by the event and the energy it provides. Even after management has made its conclusions, some will continue the fight, pursuing their own objectives.

Additional detail regarding the intervention team can be found in Chapter 6.

Step 1: Consider the eleven statements in the context of your workplace. Give your honest response by circling the appropriate number.

1 = Strongly Disagree   5 = Strongly Agree

1. The people I work with encourage each other.
    1   2   3   4   5

2. We look for ways to help each other.
    1   2   3   4   5

3. We respect different viewpoints.
    1   2   3   4   5

4. We are creative in finding solutions when working through disagreements.
    1   2   3   4   5

5. We share our knowledge so that each person can be more successful.
    1   2   3   4   5

6. We ask for input about our performance from each other: associates and customers.
    1   2   3   4   5

7. We believe in continuous improvement and our actions reflect this belief.
    1   2   3   4   5

8. We are actively in charge of our behavior and we direct ourselves toward our mission.
    1   2   3   4   5

9. We learn from our mistakes.
    1   2   3   4   5

Reflections
Reflections

10. We don't waste time affixing blame.
    1 2 3 4 5

11. We eliminate outdated policies, procedures, and methods.
    1 2 3 4 5

Scoring:
* A total of 44 or more indicates a strong environment for coping with concerns and creating positive change. Most conflicts can be dealt with at stage one levels.
* Scores below 33 signal significant work to be done. Stage one conflicts are rare; but stage two and stage three problems are frequent.

Step 2: Have each member of your team or department complete this same assessment. Review the results and compare individual perceptions. Outline a plan to improve your working relationships in the weakest areas.

Reflections

Consider a current conflict situation. Complete the following Conflict Assessment Checklist to see in which stage your conflict currently is.

STAGE ONE

Yes   No

1. Are individuals willing to meet and discuss facts?
2. Is there a sense of optimism?
3. Is there a cooperative spirit?
4. Does a "live and let live" attitude typify the atmosphere?
5. Can individuals discuss issues without involving personalities?
6. Are parties able to stay focused on the present, not the past?
7. Is the language specific?
8. Are solutions the dominate focus (as opposed to blame)?

STAGE TWO

Yes   No

1. Is there a competitive attitude?
2. Is there an emphasis on winners and losers?
3. Is it hard to talk about problems without talking about people?
4. Is the language generalized?
5. Can you identify these statements:
   "They ..."
   "Everyone is ..."
   "You always ..."
   "He never ..."
6. Is there a cautious nature when issues are discussed?

Reflections

7. Can you detect a "cover-your-hind-end" attitude?
8. Do the parties make efforts to look good?

STAGE THREE
Yes   **No**
1. Are attempts being made to get rid of others?
2. Is there an intention to hurt?
3. Have obvious leaders or spokespersons emerged?
4. Is there a choosing up of sides?
5. Has corporate good become identified with a set of special interests?
6. Is there a sense of "holy mission" on the part of certain parties?
7. Is there a sense that things will never stop?
8. Has then been a loss of middle ground, allowing only black or white options?

• Evaluate your Conflict Management Strategy choices in light of what you've discovered. (Generally, your conflict is in the stage where you had the most yes answers. Be sure to keep in mind those factors resulting from the yes answers you have in the other stages as well. Real world conflicts are in a continuous state of flux and seldom fit perfectly into one stage or another.

• What would be your best approach?

• What will be your next step?

• When will you implement it?

Reflections
Reflections

4 CONFLICT MANAGEMENT STYLES

There are five universally accepted approaches to conflict management. No one approach will work in all situations. It is, therefore, important to develop the ability to use each style in appropriate situations. Some styles will be more comfortable for you than others; they fit your natural style. Your challenge is to master those styles that you find personally difficult. When you've completed this chapter, you'll be able to identify all five conflict management styles; identify situations in which each style is effective and situations where it is not; and assess your own personal conflict management style strengths and weaknesses.

Styles of Conflict Management

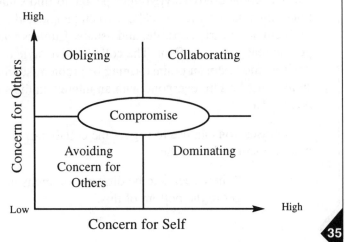

The chart illustrates five conflict styles. An individual with a knowledge of these styles can select the style most appropriate for a specific conflict. Once a style is identified, it is also possible to better understand the motivations of others during conflict

Collaboration is the win/win conflict management style. Individuals who choose this style seek an exchange of information. There is a desire to examine differences and reach a solution that is acceptable to all parties. This style is typically associated with problem-solving and is effective when issues are complex.

The collaborative style encourages creative thinking. Developing alternatives is one of the strengths of this style. Its emphasis on all parties synthesizes information from divergent perspectives. However, it is not an effective style when a party lacks commitment or when time is limited. Collaboration takes time. It can be a frustrating style during higher levels of conflict when reason and rational considerations are often overshadowed by emotional commitments to a position.

The collaborative style rallies people to find solutions to complex issues. It is excellent when people and the problem are clearly separate, and usually fruitless when people really want to fight. The collaborative style can be a positive motivator in brainstorming or problem-solving sessions. Just be sure everyone with an interest in the situation is included.

Phrases you can use to trigger the collaborative conflict management style include:

- "There seems to be different opinions here, let's get to the bottom of this."

- "Let's get several people from each department together and discuss the options."

Obliging, also called placating, is another style of conflict management. Obliging places a high value on others but a low value on self, perhaps reflecting an individual's low self-esteem. It's also a strategy that can be used to deliberately elevate another person, making them feel better about an issue. This use of obliging by raising another's status is useful, especially if your position within the company is not a politically precarious one.

The obliging strategy plays down the differences between parties while looking for common ground. The high concern for others causes an individual to satisfy and meet the needs of others, often giving up something of importance to self. Obliging, when used effectively, can preserve a relationship. Obliging used unconsciously can create instant doormats with the words boldly printed, "Please walk over me."

This style is useful if a manager is unsure of a position or fears a mistake has been made. By using the obliging style, the manager passively accepts the power of others, buying time to assess situations, and survey alternatives.

The obliging style gives power to others. If you've got expendable power, it can build trust and confidence in others. If you are secure in your position, it can be used as a method of delegation. Phrases that signal the obliging style include:

- "I don't care, whatever you want."

- "You're the expert, what do you think?"

Dominating is the opposite of obliging. The emphasis is placed on self. Whereas the obliging individual may neglect his own needs, the dominating style overlooks the needs of others. It is an effective strategy when a quick decision is needed or if a matter is unimportant.

This strategy can be reactionary, activated by self-preservation. It is reflected during an attack championed by the philosophy, "It is better to shoot at 'em than be shot at." When an issue is important, a dominating style will force others to pay attention to a specific set of needs.

The dominating style is used effectively when there is a great disparity of expertise. The ability to marshal the facts, boldly assess issues, provide expert counsel, and generate action during conflict can be invaluable. However, the flip side of direct action is incorrect action. Misplaced power can undermine future success. The dominating style is also most frequently associated with the bully and the "hardball tactics" of power brokers.

It is best to use this strategy sparingly. It lasts only as long as you have right and might on your side. Companies with a strong chain of command tend to favor this style. It usually delineates clearly where the buck stops and who holds responsibility. If you work in a system that frequently manages people and conflict with a dominating style, you'll recognize "cover-your-hind-end" thinking as a back-up strategy.

Phrases that indicate the dominating style:

- "I don't care, just do what I asked you to do."

- "It doesn't matter. That's the way it is."

Avoiding is the fourth conflict management style. The avoider does not place a high value on either self or others. This is a "don't-rock-the-boat" style.

The negative aspects of the avoiding style include passing the buck or sidestepping an issue. An individual using this style will withdraw from the events, leaving others to struggle with the results.

When issues are not important, deferring action allows things to cool off — an effective use of avoidance. It is also an effective style when time is needed. For example, during a board meeting an item can be tabled or a postponement set.

On the other hand, this style can be frustrating for others because answers are slow in developing. Little satisfaction stems from the avoiding style, and conflict tends to run its own course when the avoiding style is used.

The avoidance style buys time. Use it wisely. If you notice an individual using this style, it should be a clue that the other person is uncertain and needs time to investigate the situation. Above all, make it a point to follow up once time is granted. Conflict usually does not go away with time.

Phrases that signal the avoiding style include:

- "Can we put this on hold temporarily?"

- "I haven't seen all the facts, I'll get back to you when ..."

Do you have an avoider working with you? Are you wondering how to get an issue moving? Here are some coping mechanisms and reminders:

- You cannot care about people who do not care for themselves! You can sympathize, love, and cajole, but the avoider must have enough concern for self or others before significant movement can take place.

- Communicate your enthusiasm and hopes. Avoid the negative. Overcome the forces of inactivity by moving in a positive direction.

- Let them off the hook. Separate the people from the problem for them. Provide a focus on the problem.

- Play on the avoider's sense of honesty. Seek out and define the reasons for resistance and inactivity.

- Limit the number of variables presented to the avoider. Place one issue on an agenda; remove others. Make a decision easier by eliminating distractions.

- Set a deadline.

Compromising is another conflict management style. It is pictured in the center of the Five Conflict Styles chart at the beginning of this chapter —rating neither high nor low in concern for others or self. This is a middle-of-the-road orientation. In compromise, everyone has something to give and something to take. It is powerful when both sides are right. It errs when one side is wrong!

The compromise is most effective as a tool when issues are complex or when there is a balance of power. Compromise can be chosen when other methods have failed and both parties are ready to clarify polarities and look for middle ground. Compromise may mean splitting the difference or exchanging concessions. It almost always means all parties give up something in order to attain resolution.

Negotiation and bargaining are complementary skills to the compromise style. The advantage of compromise is that it gets parties talking about the issues and hopefully moves them closer together. It will always be difficult to maintain impartiality, and you can expect to be accused of favoritism when this style is used. Rarely can business afford winners and losers, so use this style only when the losses can be minimized for both sides!

When embarking on a compromise, ask both parties to thoughtfully answer these four questions:

1. What is the minimum I can accept?

2. What is the maximum I can go for without getting thrown out of the room?

3. What is the maximum I can give up?

4. What is the least I can offer without getting thrown out of the room?

Stage one and even stage two conflict can employ compromise with some success, but once stage three has been reached, all parties may see a compromise as making them losers and seek retribution either overtly or through another situation down the road.

Phrases that indicate a compromising approach include:

- "I can see we have differing opinions. What's your bottom line?"

- "We all have to give and take if we're going to work together, so let's put things on the table."

The five styles of conflict management provide a structure for action. A knowledge of these styles increases your understanding of conflict and of your own conflict management style.

Factors Affecting Your Approach

K Knowledge:

- How much do you know about the other person's issue?

- How much does the other person know about your issue?

- How familiar are you with the subject?

- Do you have knowledge that the other person doesn't have?

A Authority:

- Do you have the authority to make a decision?

- Does the other person have authority to make a decision?

P Power:

- How much leverage can you bring to bear on the situation?

- How much power does the other person have over you? (Remember: Knowledge is power.)

O Others:

- How important is the relationship to you?

- How important is the relationship to the other person?

W Winning:

- How important is the aspect of winning?

- Do you have to win?

- Does the other party have to win?

- Is compromise acceptable?

- Is losing acceptable?

Handling Conflict the ACES Way

A   **Assess** the situation.

C   **Clarify** the issues.

E   **Evaluate** alternative approaches.

S   **Solve** the problem.

Conflict Management Style Survey

Rank items A through E for each item. Place the number 5 next to the best response for you, then 4 for the next best, then 3, then 2, then 1 for the least accurate one. Try not to agonize over these. There are no right or wrong answers, only truthful ones. Generally, your initial gut response is the most accurate one. Make your choices quickly. You must rank all 5 choices for each question — even those with whichyou struggle with.

1. When you have strong feelings in a conflict situation, you would:

_____ A. Enjoy the emotional release and sense of exhilaration and accomplishment.

_____ B. Enjoy the challenge of the conflict.

_____ C. Become serious and concerned about how others are feeling and thinking.

_____ D. Find it frightening because someone will get hurt.

_____ E. Become convinced there is nothing you can do to resolve the issue.

2. What's the best result you can expect from a conflict?

_____ A. Conflict helps people face facts.

_____ B. Conflict cancels out extremes in thinking so a strong middle ground can be reached.

_____ C. Conflict clears the air, enhances commitment and results.

_____ D. Conflict demonstrates the absurdity of self-centeredness and draws people closer together.

_____ E. Conflict lessens complacency and assigns blame where it belongs.

Reflections

3. **When you have authority in a conflict situation, you would:**

_____ A. Put it straight and let others know your view.

_____ B. Try to negotiate the best settlement.

_____ C. Ask for other viewpoints and suggest that a position be found that both sides might try.

_____ D. Go along with the others, providing support where you can.

_____ E. Keep the encounter impersonal, citing rules if they apply.

4. **When someone takes an unreasonable position, you would:**

_____ A. Lay it on the line and say that you don't like it.

_____ B. Let him or her know in casual, subtle ways that you're not pleased; possibly distract with humor; and avoid direct confrontation.

_____ C. Call attention to the conflict and explore mutually acceptable solutions.

_____ D. Keep your misgivings to yourself.

_____ E. Let your actions speak for you, possibly using depression or lack of interest.

5. **When you become angry with a peer, you:**

_____ A. Explode without giving it much thought.

_____ B. Smooth things over with a good story.

_____ C. Express your anger and invite a response.

_____ D. Compensate for your anger by acting the opposite of your feelings.

_____ E. Remove yourself from the situation.

6. **When you find yourself disagreeing with other members about a project, you:**

_____ A. Stand by your convictions and defend them.

Reflections
Reflections

_____ B. Appeal to the logic of the group in the hope of convincing at least a majority you are right.

_____ C. Explore points of agreement and disagreement, then search for alternatives that take everyone's views into account.

_____ D. Go along with the group.

_____ E. Do not participate in the discussion and don't feel bound by any decision made.

7. When one group member takes a position in opposition to the rest of the group, you would:

_____ A. Point out publicly that the dissenting member is blocking the group and suggest that the group move on without him or her if necessary.

_____ B. Make sure the dissenting member has a chance to communicate his or her objections so that a compromise can be reached.

_____ C. Try to uncover why the dissenting member views that issue differently so that the group's members can re-evaluate their own positions.

_____ D. Encourage members to set the conflict aside and go on to more agreeable items on the agenda.

_____ E. Remain silent because it is best to avoid becoming involved.

8. When you see conflict emerging in your team, you would:

_____ A. Push for a quick decision to ensure that the task is completed.

_____ B. Avoid outright confrontation by moving the discussion toward a middle ground.

_____ C. Share with the group your impression of what is going on so that the nature of the impending

Reflections

conflict can be discussed.

_____ D. Relieve the tension with humor.

_____ E. Stay out of the conflict as long as it is of no concern to you.

9. In handling conflict between group members, you would:

_____ A. Anticipate areas of resistance and prepare responses to objections prior to open conflict.

_____ B. Encourage your members to be prepared by identifying in advance areas of possible compromise.

_____ C. Recognize that conflict is healthy and press for the identification of shared concerns and/or goals.

_____ D. Promote harmony on the grounds that the only real result of conflict is the destruction of friendly relations.

_____ E. Submit the issue to an impartial arbitrator.

10. In your view, what might be the reason for the failure of one group to work with another?

_____ A. Lack of a clearly stated position or failure to back up the group's position.

_____ B. Tendency of groups to force their leaders to abide by the group's decision, as opposed to promoting flexibility, which would facilitate compromise.

_____ C. Tendency of groups to enter negotiations with a win/lose perspective.

_____ D. Lack of motivation on the part of the group's leaders, resulting in the leaders placing emphasis on maintaining their own power positions rather than addressing the issues involved.

_____ E. Irresponsible behavior on the part of the group's leaders, resulting in the leaders placing emphasis on maintaining their own power positions rather than addressing the issues involved.

Scoring:

Go back and total the numbers you have placed for each letter and record the totals below. (Add up all the numbers for A and record. Then add all the numbers for B, etc.) For example, if you had placed the number 5 next to A for all 10 questions, your score for A would be 50.

A _____   D _____

B _____   E _____

C _____

Column A: Dominating Style
Column B: Compromising Style
Column C: Collaborative Style
Column D: Obliging Style
Column E: Avoiding Style

Look at your totals.

• The highest number typically represents the conflict management style you perceive yourself to use most. (Most people see themselves as collaborators.)

• Look at the second highest number. It typically more accurately represents your strongest conflict management style.

• The lowest number represents the style in which your skills are typically the weakest.

Outline a plan to strengthen your weakest conflict management style.

Reflections

5 CONSTRUCTIVE MANAGEMENT STYLES

Whether the issue is boardroom planning or conflict on the production line, to be an effective conflict manager, you must develop a deliberate decision-making process around company goals. When you've completed this chapter you will have these additional tools in your conflict management arsenal: five principles for maintaining positive relationships during conflict; numerous ways to enhance passive, aggressive, and manipulative conflict management styles; and ten tips for dealing with angry employees.

Maintaining Positive Relationships During Conflict

Managers set the climate for employees. Trust, openness, and shared responsibility are essential to effectively dealing with the inevitable organizational conflict. Anger within the organization can either propel it forward or destroy its ability to function. The way managers deal with conflict and anger plays a critical role in determining which it will be.

To make the best decisions during conflict, managers need a healthy understanding of relationships. Here are five principles for maintaining positive relationships during conflict.

Encourage Equal Participation

Shared responsibility increases ownership. Higher stages of conflict cause individuals to become destructive and lose sight of the organization in favor of personal issues. A simple reminder that "we" are a team can often encourage the desired ownership. You can also share the leadership responsibility by expecting team members to think like a manager in the situation, asking for creative responses to events that promote cooperation rather than split decisions.

Other examples of shared responsibility include subdividing tasks that generate deliberate barriers of responsibility, and then requiring team leaders to cross the barriers by providing assignments that require cooperative efforts.

Author Thomas Peter's fervor about the need for a service-oriented management style applies during conflict:

"We must fundamentally shift our managerial philosophy from adversarial to cooperative. It is vital to engage in multi-function problem-solving and to target business systems that cross several functional boundaries. Ford and IBM both say they wasted years before realizing that most quality improvement opportunities lie outside the natural work group."

The importance of shared responsibility is to make the point, emphatically, that no one person owns a problem and everyone shares in the responsibility for solving sticky issues.

Actively Listen

Listening skills are inexpensive to obtain yet priceless when acquired. People are constantly talking, but too often never stop to listen. Poor listening is the #1 cause of conflict. It's the #1 cause of work having to be done and redone before it meets the stated requirements. Listening is a two-way street. Before a manager can expect his subordinates to listen to him, he must demonstrate the skill by truly listening to his people.

Listening affirms others in several ways:

(1) Listening says you are important, and I'll take time to hear what you have to say.

(2) Listening provides quick access to a perspective on conflict.

(3) Listening provides data for the manager to make decisions.

(4) Listening builds relationships.

Many people are uncomfortable with silence. The effective manager knows that taking time to listen, even if there are periods of silence, is an investment in the relationship. Here are just a few of the things you can do to fill the silence while tending to the other party:

• Watch the individual's eyes.

• Learn to read body language.

• Listen intently to the words and listen between the lines. What is the tone of voice telling you? Do the words match the body language?

• Test yourself after visiting with others. Did you gain as much information as you gave out?

Take the time to sharpen your listening skills. Use audio tapes and desktop reference materials to build and maintain this critical skill.

Take Time to Step Back

A moratorium can be declared over issues, problems, or decisions. The manager uses time as a resource, deliberately stating intentions and working behind the scenes to ensure the greatest possible outcome. These suggestions could be used to introduce a moratorium:

"We have some time; let's meet in small groups and look for alternatives."

"No decision is worth hurt feelings. There are several people who have spent company time and proposed quality ideas. I want to find out why there is such diversity of opinion."

"The amount of time and energy that have been spent on this issue are significant. We're not ready to decide. Now that we've seen the issues a little more time invested at this point might help everyone."

The declaration of a moratorium is a valuable tool. Taking this step back can give all parties the opportunity to regain their objectivity and reassess their position and consider the long-term impact this conflict may have on their working relationships with colleagues and co-workers.

Overall, relationships are more important than decisions. Roger Fisher, in *Getting Together* says, "If we want a relationship that can deal with serious differences, we have to improve the process itself, independent of the particular substantive problems involved." Time taken to ensure this principle builds a healthy foundation that can tolerate intense conflict.

Steven Covey, in his landmark books *The Seven Habits of Highly Effective People* and *First Things First*, speaks of relationships as emotional bank accounts. Continual deposits into the account by making commitments and keeping them, listening to and affirming others, building trust, and creating rapport are required so a conflict does not bankrupt the relationship.

Differentiate Fact from Opinion

It is easy to believe your position is the truth. Far too often, however, positions reflect perceptions rather than reality. If you challenge categorical statements and encourage conditional truth, you will be more effective during higher levels of conflict because the very issues of stage two and stage three deal with perceptions.

Conditional truth is a philosophical acceptance that the position any person takes is accurate and in the best interest of the company. When we develop a "conditional truth" orientation, it grants every participant the opportunity to be correct and the right to be heard before conclusions are drawn or decisions made. Conditional truth is more of an attitude than a process. The effective manager instills a questioning attitude that looks for alternatives rather than debate.

If you take strong leadership at this point, conflict becomes a matter of separating perspectives rather than challenging liars, a difficult task with adults. But be cautious; a stage two conflict escalates quickly. Your staff will be ready to blame and accuse rather than work toward resolution, causing a distortion of facts. Conditional thinking will make it harder for individuals to "own" positions.

Separating fact from opinion also enhances creativity. Individuals conditioned to consider alternative perspectives are less likely to settle for pat answers. During confrontation they are more likely to evaluate multiple options as a part of their standard operating procedure.

Focus on the Problem — Not the People

This strategy is essential to appropriately manage conflict at any stage. When the people and the problem are tangled together, a problem takes on an entirely new dimension usually typified by volatility.

It is frequently difficult to separate the people from the problem, but as a manager you must! Some ideas that can help you separate people from the problem include:

- Talk in specific rather than general terms.

- Use concrete terms and ask for facts.

- Challenge assumptions.

- Address conflicting parties as if they have no information. This provides an opportunity for them to hear a perspective without having to defend their territory, separating them from the event for a moment.

- Create a safe environment. The flight/fight response is activated during high stages of conflict. Safety enhances the possibilities that individuals will move away from protracted positions.

- Speak in the passive rather than the active voice. For example, you might say, "A problem was created when (whatever happened)" as opposed to "You cause a problem when you (whatever)."

- Do a role reversal where opposing parties play each other's role in the conversation.

Nine Steps for Building Cooperation

- Clearly define the problem

- Look for commonalities

- Respect all contributions — no matter how lame

- Recognize multiple interests

- Respect all individuals in words and manners

- Look toward solutions

- Move from WIIFM (what's in it for me) to WIIFU (what's in it for us)

- Focus on benefits

- Allow time to evaluate and make decisions

Leading From Strength

Corporate America has excellent role models and out-standing business innovators. They know what to do and when to do it! But they are the exception. Whether it is fear of accountability or a general lack of confidence, many of us lack a sense of direction and purpose, especially during conflict. The tools you need to manage conflict are the same management tools you use daily in business. Effective management must be deliberate and move toward a measurable product. Conflict management, although possibly more intimidating, requires this same basic management orientation. Conflict calls for the most deliberate and strategic actions you make as a manager.

People look for decisive action during conflict. You appear decisive when you have specific goals and objectives. You must manage the affairs of your company from a position of strength, knowing and then doing what is best to meet your stated purpose.

Strong leadership is confident, assertive, and balanced. A good manager accepts and even welcomes diverse perspectives and alternative viewpoints. The powerful executive is one who has a solid management philosophy and is not unduly threatened by the presence of competing philosophies.

A Passive Management Style

Weak leadership is frequently passive. The problem with passive management is glossing over things and a loss of respect from co-workers. A passive style is more effective at lower stages of conflict because the coping strategies of avoidance and obliging tend to be passive in nature. If you have a reputation for being indecisive and have a passive management style, the actions you take during higher levels of conflict will probably look feeble to others.

However, the natural characteristics of the passive style can be an asset. The passive style provides an appearance of being distant and unaffected, although the passive manager is usually frustrated with intense conflict. This outward appearance of calm can be settling to others, but the passive manager must communicate that he is addressing the issues.

While fear, anxiety, and guilt can make any manager ineffective, the passive manager may feel completely out of control. Enhancing self confidence is critical to the passive manager developing effective conflict management skills.

These statements typify the passive manager and may cause a counter-productive reaction:

- I wish ...

- If only ...

- I'm sorry but ...

- This is probably wrong ...

The following five ideas can help convert a passive style to a more effective style.

1. Communicate face-to-face whenever possible. This demonstrates involvement.

2. Don't respond quickly with agreement. Take some time, even if you don't need it.

3. Interrupt and ask clarifying or probing questions. Be part of the event.

4. Watch for guilt. Guilt is an early warning sign that insecurities exist and that the conflict requires management skills beyond the passive style.

5. Evaluate how a conflict fits into the overall direction a department is moving — the big picture.

Barriers to Conflict Resolution

- Discounting the entire message when one flaw is found

- Judging the messenger rather than evaluating the message

- Scanning your arguments

- Giving premature responses

- Listening for agreement rather than for understanding

- Wandering mind

- Drive to be right

- The "principle of it"

#1   #2   #3

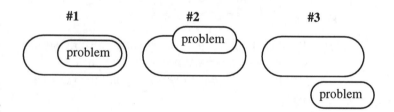

The problem might be part of the big picture, as in #1. Possibly the conflict is only one aspect of the "big picture," as in drawing #2. At other times, the conflict is not related to the "big picture," as in drawing #3. Where the conflict fits will help determine the appropriate actions to be taken.

Aggressive and Manipulative Management Styles

Aggressive and manipulative management styles are not particularly effective in conflict management either. An aggressive style might be decisive (desirable) but is also dictatorial (not desirable). Aggressive and manipulative management styles are frequently reflections of internal insecurities such as being unsure of one's value, attitudes and personal commitments. These styles are ineffective because they reduce trust and place self-interest above others, leading to serious credibility problems.

Aggression is a defense mechanism triggered during conflict and tends to prompt equally aggressive responses, which then escalate the conflict. Aggressive managers can be perceived as capricious, making decision with no real cause or foundation. When you sense aggression, examine the underlying issues:

- Is this a common reaction in these situations?

- Do you have a point to prove or an ax to grind?

- Is this energy properly directed for the event?

- Do other people have the same reaction?

Closely akin to aggression is anger. Anger is a secondary emotion; an initial emotion precedes it. For example, someone questions the quality of your work and you respond in anger but your primary emotion was that you felt your abilities were being belittled.

There are times when anger and aggression are important and useful at work. For example, if you must deal with a difficult person and the event requires firm, clear intentions, aggression can be an ally. But this aggressive style should be consciously chosen, not result from a reactive emotion.

Ten Tips for Dealing with Aggressive, Angry Employees

1. Remember to share the responsibility. It's hard to be combative with someone who's on your side.

2. Encourage listening; be informed. It's amazing how much you can discover if you tend to the words of others.

3. Pay attention to excessive self-interest. Winning is for everyone.

4. A title or position within a company may grant control over people, but true authority involves respect. Respect must be earned. Dictatorial leadership is not conducive to a team philosophy. Seek suggestions from the others.

5. Anger is short-lived for most aggressive people. There are individuals, however, who don't forget. Enemies created during the resolution of one conflict may be around for the next. Is that happening here?

6. Deal with the situation immediately — not later today, not next week. Do it now. Many performance problems reach crisis proportions as a result of delays in dealing with anger.

7. Allow the employees to talk. Listen. Don't interrupt. They want to be heard. Be sure you understand their position before stating yours.

8. If anger is expressed in a staff meeting, ask the angry employee if he would like to discuss it now (publicly) or later (privately). Let him call the shots.

9. Deal with the employee's feelings first. Then address the underlying issue. "I can tell you're really annoyed. I'd like to hear what you have to say." When the discussion is concluding, check the feelings again to be sure they've been resolved. Ask him if he is satisfied or feels better. Be alert to tone of voice and non-verbal cues as you may not get a completely honest answer. If your employee is still upset, let it pass for now. Staying upset a bit longer may allow your employee to save face and justify his initial angry response.

10. If the employee declines to discuss what's troubling him, try, "I understand you're hesitant to discuss this, but we'd both be better off to get it out in the open. Let's come back to this tomorrow." Be sure to follow up.

- Do you feel confident about the situation?

- Do you understand the company and its policies well enough to respond as a manager?

- If you are wrong, is there room to learn from your errors?

- Are you willing to allow outsiders to help you in the conflict?

- Do you find yourself asserting your point of view more often than listening to others?

- Do you worry a great deal about how you look to others? If so, it can be a sign of self-focus rather than team orientation.

- When team members have a good idea, do you sell them to top management as your own?

- Do you tend to identify team members as expendable commodities that can be pushed and pulled in the manner that best suits a set of goals without regard to their input?

- Do you develop a genuine atmosphere of satisfaction?

- Would you want to work for a boss just like you?

Reflections

6 COMMUNICATION'S CONTRIBUTIONS TO CONFLICT

Conflict perceived to be rooted in action and content is often caused by communication failures. Communication can be a major problem. Many issues could be resolved if only communication was improved. When you've completed this chapter, you'll have an understanding of the complexities of communication, ways to make your communication more positive, a model for constructive confrontation, and other techniques to simplify your conflict communications.

The Interpersonal Communication Gap

Poor communication compounds problems as individuals begin to project what they believe are the other side's motivations. This gap between intended messages and received messages contributes to communication problems during conflict.

Getting on the Same "Wavelength"

People tend to prefer one of three sensory modes — especially under stress. The language people use is your clue to sensory mode preference. Use their language to get on the same wavelength, to match perceptions, and to avoid a mismatch in communication.

Visual (pictures)
look * see * picture * focus * view * observe
perspective * feature * show * demonstrate * apparent
appearance

Auditory (sounds)
hear * listen * tone * sounds * tune * note * ring
buzz * say * explain * loud and clear * tell * clamor
noisy

Kinesthetic (touch)
feel * sense * grasp * smooth * warm * cold * rough
touch * hold * clutch * run with it * grab hold of it

The Interpersonal Gap

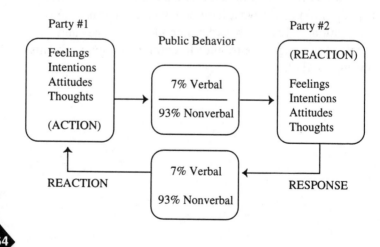

Only 7% of communication is actually transmitted verbally. The remaining 93% is nonverbal. Facial expressions, body language, and the tone of voice play a significant role in our conversations with others. Difficulties arise as individuals struggle to match the other party's words and actions, with the perceived motivations, attitudes, and feelings that already exist.

It is not surprising so much conflict is based on miscommunication. It's actually amazing that we understand each other as often as we do.

One factor that makes the interpersonal gap more complex is the use of inadequate conflict strategies. The avoidance style employed as a coping mechanism can be interpreted incorrectly. What is intended as toleration of peculiarities might be perceived as annoyance or lack of concern. A daily irritation becomes a problem equaling a stage one conflict.

In another instance, rather than debate an insignificant issue, one party might give in by using the obliging style. Party two, assuming a lack of commitment, takes offense. If there has been a history of poor communication, party one might become "one of those people who never cares," and the beginnings of a stage two conflict appear.

Words improperly used or vain attempts to spare another's feelings also fall into this interpersonal gap. When an emotion does not match the explanation, the possibility for conflict increases greatly. No one can accurately send or receive communication 100% of the time, which in itself is reason for having a conflict management strategy. Conflict is inevitable given the dynamics of communication.

Whether your method of communication is verbal, or written, face-to-face, or long-distance, the way you express yourself will affect whether or not your message is well received. Reduce your communication-based conflicts by embracing these steps.

1. Eliminate negative language: Negative language conveys a poor image. It, alone, causes conflict and confrontation where none is necessary. It can have a subtle tone of blame, or be interpreted as sarcastic or patronizing.

    Negative language focuses on what cannot be done and ignores positive actions or consequences. Common negative words/phrases include expressions that imply carelessness, untruths, or ignorance. Furthermore, negative language can be demanding and overgeneralized. Negative language includes:

can't	claim
won't	should
unable to	ought to
neglected	must
failed	always
ignored	never

2. Replace the negative with positive language that focuses on what can be done, alternatives, and choices. Positive language stresses positive actions and consequences rather than anticipating negative ones. Positive language includes:

If ... then	welcome
suggest	agree
viewpoint	benefit
perspective	"I" statements
option	excellent

10 Tips for Handling the Predictable Hassles

When People You Work With:	Ideas:
• Push your hot buttons	Have a humorous response
• Make a rude, personal statement	Agree *"You're right."*
• Make an outrageous accusation	Silence, then redirect *"Speaking of..., did you...?"*
• Are complaining of troubles	Reflect back what you hear
• Blame you when it is not your fault	Acknowledge *"I am sorry about...."* And act *"How can I help?"*
• Won't stop arguing	Agree to disagree and move on
• Are in dead-end discussions	Sidestep *"Let's come back to this later."*
• Are pressing you for a decision	Acknowledge what is happening *"You aren't pushing me, are you?"*
• Keep asking questions	Answer with a question *"What do you mean?"*
• Are belaboring a point	Switch the conversation *"That reminds me..."*

The Constructive Confrontation Model

When addressing problem situations and/or behaviors, the flow of language will really set the tone. To place the issues on the table for discussion in a non-threatening fashion, use this four-step, straightforward communication tool.

1. Use an "I" statement to specify your reaction to the problem.

"I get angry ..."

"I am frustrated ..."

If you want to soften the approach even further, switch to an "It is" statement.

It is annoying ...

2. Specify the inappropriate behavior to be stopped.

    "... when you interrupt ..."

    "... when you yell ..."

    "... when you come in late ..."

3. State the reason for your reaction.

    "... because I lose my train of thought."

    "... because I don't know how to handle it."

    "... because I have to do your work."

4. Specify the behavior you want instead.

    "Therefore, please let me finish before you give me your input."

    "Therefore, please lower your voice so we can continue this conversation."

    "Therefore, please be at your desk no later than 8:00 in the morning."

    Even if you think it's obvious what the replacement behavior should be, spell it out anyway. You need to finish all four steps to close the loop for this tool to work effectively.

This low key approach will work well in most instances of low level conflict. You may need to repeat the process from time to time as a reminder. Don't expect the other person's behavior to radically change overnight. It may well take time for the new behavior to truly take hold.

The Broken Record Technique

If you have repeatedly tried to use the constructive confrontation model with a particular individual about a specific behavior and seen no willingness to change or cooperate, you may need to move to a more direct style: The Broken Record Technique.

With this technique you repeat your statement verbatim over and over again until the other person finally gets it. For example, say you're dealing with someone who persists on interrupting you despite your efforts to moderate to get him to modify his behavior. Try this: When he interrupts you, interrupt him with:

"You interrupted me" and proceed with what you have to say. When he interrupts you again, say it again.

"You interrupted me." Again ...

"You interrupted me."

Repeat your confrontational statement over and over in a pleasant, soft voice until the person finally stops interrupting you. After three or four repetitions, you may well begin to feel foolish but don't worry. You're making a point.

You must outlast the other person for this technique to work. If you're not willing to hang in there for however long it takes, do not begin the broken record technique.

The worst thing you can do is to start it and give in in the middle. When you do that, you've just told the other person, "If you persist in your inappropriate behavior long enough, you'll win."

Defending Yourself From a Verbal Attack

Many people both colleagues and customers alike use angry behavior to control you and the interaction. Be sure to avoid arguing and threatening by carefully monitoring your own behavior. Don't take the hostile bait.

- Wait a few seconds before responding.

- Speak slowly and softly.

- Take a time out if you're getting angry.

- Show that the complaint and feelings are important.

- Treat the person as a valued individual.

- Help them see options and choices.

- Use non-inflammatory words and body language.

- Watch your facial expressions and your tone of voice.

- Ask, "When did you start thinking that ... ?"

- Change the subject slightly. Move to a related area.

- Actively solicit feedback about your own communication and communication within the organization. Ask questions such as:

  "When we talk, are you generally clear about what I am saying?"

  "Do you think we communicate well?"

  "What ideas do you have about how we could communicate better?"

- Review a recent memo you wrote looking for positive vs. negative language.

- Listen to yourself as you speak with colleagues, coworkers and family members. Do you usually use positive language, or have you fallen into the negative language trap? What specific negative words or phrases could you begin to eliminate from your common usage?

- Think of two situations in which you can use the Constructive Confrontation Model this week. Prepare exactly what you want to say. Schedule a time to address each of these issues.

- Practice the Broken Record Technique on one of your children this week. Then try it, when appropriate, at work.

Reflections

7 EMOTIONAL ASPECTS OF CONFLICT

Emotions are an integral part of conflict. They need to be fully understood to facilitate appropriate responses to various conflicts. When you've completed this chapter, you'll have a list of questions to moderate your reactions while a conflict is in its infancy, as well as a full understanding of stress patterns (emotional response continuum) and reflexes (emotional reflexology). Additionally, you'll have five powerful "don'ts" to rely upon during a conflict.

How to Stay Cool, Calm and in Control ... Most of the Time

Question #1: "Is this event or situation pushing one of my hot buttons?"

A hot button is anything that makes you see red and makes your temper flare automatically. Perhaps a certain tone of voice or facial expression sets you off or maybe certain words get under your skin immediately. These occur because of past experiences carried forward in your mind and emotions. Is one of these internal triggers being activated in this situation or are you truly reacting to this singular conflict? Pause to answer this question before reacting.

Question #2: "What is my level of commitment to this person or event?"

If this is a situation that will not recur or is with someone you will never see again, just how much time and emotional energy is worth investing in this situation? Why get embroiled in this matter at all? Reserve yourself for those issues that really matter.

On the other hand, if this matter is of great consequence or if it is a conflict with a person who will remain an integral part of your life, tempering your response may be desirable. Allowing yourself to become emotionally embroiled in a controversy without thinking through the potential long-term consequences of your words and actions is probably not in your best interest. Pause. Take a deep breath. Think about the importance of your relationship with this individual and then respond.

Question #3: "What else is happening right now in my life?"

Your overall stress level makes a big difference in how you handle difficulties at any point in time. What types of major life stressors do you have? How secure do you feel in your job? What is the state of your marriage? Your interactions with your children? All these major undercurrents of stress will dramatically impact your ability to cope calmly with conflict situations.

Suppose your life is great. You don't have any major stressors right now. Does that automatically mean that nothing else is having an impact on your conflict resolution skills? Absolutely not. Even smaller, short-term irritants can cause major differences in responses. For example, you get up for work early one morning and you feel great! You just got a raise, your spouse is appreciative of you, and you just have the world by the tail! You are a 10! You run into the kitchen and start the coffee. You jump into the shower and one of the kids left a bar of soap in the bottom of the tub. You fall and bruise your tailbone. You are now an 8.

When you've finished your shower, you go back to the kitchen to get that much needed cup of coffee. Uh-oh! You started the coffee but you forgot to put the pot under the drip and you now have coffee all over the kitchen counter and floor. You are now a 4.

Cleaning up the kitchen has made you late and you still haven't had that much needed cup of coffee. Nevertheless, you jump into your clothes and bolt out the front door. Some idiot cuts you off as you enter the highway and scares you witless. You are now a 2. As you run into your office building, you are greeted by a colleague with "Hi, I'm glad you got here. I need you to do this for me right away!"

Chances are this person will not receive the calm, calculated response you would make under normal circumstances. The stressful events of the morning have clouded your ability to cope and have shaped the type of reaction you will have to any request or demand.

Therefore, always be sure to evaluate what else is happening in your life that might be affecting your reactions and responses in difficult situations. If you find other stressors prevalent at that time, take a step back and separate the specific conflict in question in order to give a reasonable, appropriate response.

Question #4: "On a scale of 1 - 10, just how important is this?"

Not all differences of opinion or approach are of sufficient consequence to warrant discussion and negotiation. All too often, many people will argue their position with great passion regardless of the significance of the issue at hand.

Stepping back and determining how important an issue this is will help you differentiate those conflicts worth pursuing from those better left unchallenged.

Equally effective, is to ask the other individual involved in the conflict the same question. "On a scale of 1 - 10, just how important is this to you?" If it is of no great consequence to either of you (4 or less), which approach you take is really not important. Pick one. Flip a coin. Draw straws. Use whatever system is most expeditious.

- If one of you finds the issue important (6 or more) and the other declares it of little consequence (4 or less), the approach taken should be that of the one to whom the issue holds great importance. Only if both parties find the issue of consequence (6 or more) should detailed discussions and negotiations take place.

The Emotional Response Continuum

People follow a predictable sequence in an attempt to deal with the emotional aspects of conflict called the rejection response.

- Phase 1: Anxiety

- Phase 2: Acceptance

- Phase 3: Internal Inventory

- Phase 4: Balanced Reflection

Phase 1: Anxiety

Anxiety is a natural response to change and conflict. Concerns about worth, values, and safety are activated. Some people hide this response; others become transparent.

Robert Bridges, in his book *Transitions*, makes a point that every beginning is preceded by an ending. Even birth, the starting point of life, is preceded by the ending of a symbiotic relationship between fetus and mother. During conflict everyone adjusts to transitions, both the endings and beginnings.

Our anxiety is often encased in fear, and fear is a powerful motivator. It can move an individual away from anxiety toward action. This fear response may or may not be measurable, but it is there! Some people will dig in their heels and protect their present security levels, while others will risk change and explore alternatives. If intervention strategies are to be effective, it must be understood that conflict initially prompts anxiety. Some respond to this anxiety as if it is only a minor irritation (stage one), but others will protect their comfort zone and fight (stage three).

Phase 2: Acceptance

Individuals will reach the acceptance level once the anxiety has passed. A major void exists between anxiety and acceptance, and many conflicts never bridge this gap.

When a person experiences anxiety, one response is to reject the other party. The strength of a relationship is tested at this point, with values clarified and common points of interest examined. One possible conclusion is that the relationship is not worth sustaining. Conflict is resolved by accepting the loss of a relationship.

A more desired conclusion is an acceptance that things can be dealt with; the people and the products are worth the struggle. Acceptance generates a question of survival reflected in the question, "What's in this for me," followed by an issue of winners and losers. Relationships that produce losers eventually create an unhealthy organization stuck in a cycle of hurt and be hurt, with a weak commitment among the members.

In conflict, individuals must move away from blame. This movement prompts acceptance. At times acceptance develops slowly, possibly too slowly for some, adding additional stress to the events. But once a level of acceptance is attained, the next step in the rejection response follows quite naturally.

Phase 3: Internal Inventory

The internal inventory involves weighing values and concerns, with each involved party deciding whether it is time to fight, stand up for one's values and concerns, or retreat and wait for a better time. Some psychologists suggest this inventory is triggered by self-concept (how an individual inherently views oneself). Others believe it is an instinct that happens in a fleeting moment based on survival. Whatever the motivation, it is the growing edge for both the individual and a company. Conflict presents opportunities at this phase.

The point of contact between what is and what might be is called the "growing edge." Issues of support and feelings of hopelessness arise now. Some people learn trust if adequate support is discovered, while others step toward despair, unable to find meaning or direction. Some build a world of fantasy while others construct a wall of resistance, never again to be threatened.

The responses to this internal inventory are too numerous for generalizations. It is important to apply listening skills during this time. One will identify deep feelings such as rage and anger and share personal values. The intensity and diversity of emotions can be a gold mine for a manager aware of conflict management principles. Or these emotions can seem like a snake pit if one is unprepared for conflict management.

Growth and wholeness come through the effective management of inner emotions. As a manager, you can help turn your negative emotions into positive affirmations by using this process.

1. Affirm that you are worthwhile whether raging or calm. Appreciate your anger.

2. Identify negative feelings before they are expressed. Body language is an excellent signal. Listen carefully, discern wisely, and focus consciously. Be aware of your anger.

3. Trust yourself. Feel, speak and act spontaneously. Go with the flow until you find it ineffective or unsatisfying. Trust your anger.

4. Own your thoughts, feelings, words, and actions. Others do not make me angry; I choose to be angry. Own your anger.

Phase 4: Balanced Reflection

An awareness of real-world living emerges during the final phase of the rejection response. Running from issues means continually running. Fighting never stops, and change seems to continue no matter where one draws the line. Through it all, a perspective of balance can provide an individual with a sense that things can be taken a step at a time.

Stage one conflict is handled regularly by this balanced perspective through the use of coping. Problems arise, but coping determines when and where irritations should be addressed. Stage two conflict requires management skills. It is more complex, but the balanced perspective sees conflict as an opportunity and not just a destructive force.

Stage three conflictis managed through intervention and calling on others. The balanced perspective during stage three identifies a need for outside resources and does not perceive asking for help as a weakness. The balanced perspective identifies areas where growth and possibilities exist. Timing is used effectively as each individual decides whether it is the right time for new journeys.

Emotional Reflexology

Webster provides two definitions for the word reflex: "Having a backward direction," and "Actions performed by the nervous system involuntarily." When these two definitions are combined, an excellent explanation arises for the emotional dynamic inherent in all of our reflex patterns. Given this, the emotional element of conflict can be called emotional reflexology.

Emotional reflexology is a movement away from cooperation (turning backward) that involuntarily arises when conflict escalates. Emotional reflexology is characterized by four elements:

- Blaming

- Secrecy

- Repressed feelings

- Anger

Blaming. The first tendency is to place blame. There is an almost instinctive desire to find out "who-done-it." Our Western emphasis on fairness and equality seems to automatically look for a wronged party. This emotional reaction leads away from a solution and entangles the people and the problem. The drive to place blame decreases responsibility for the problem and elevates one party over others as blameless. A dichotomized perspective arises around blame rather than solutions.

An example of this blaming response is the all too frequent finger pointing of one department against another. It is easy to identify problems; it is far more difficult to generate opportunities to solve problems once things have gone wrong. The tendency to place blame generally moves away from a solution because cover-ups and justification absorb much energy.

Secrecy. Another element of emotional reflexology is a tendency to be secretive. When facts are most needed, they tend to go underground, held as bargaining chips for later debate. This reaction is accompanied by an inability to remain neutral. Sides gather their facts around polarized positions with an attitude toward protectiveness. This encourages an element of secrecy that thwarts conflict management efforts as conflict escalates.

Most managers quickly identify with this point. People are quick to blame but slow to snitch on a fellow employee who has a drug or alcohol problem. Rumors that run rampant in the lunchroom are rarely verifiable through the best fact-finding sessions of management. The "secret" factor stifles conflict management efforts.

Repressed Feelings. A third aspect of emotional reflexology is a prevailing attitude held by many that feelings are bad and emotions should be held back. Repression of feelings, especially anger, makes provocation possible.

Emotions are a fact, and you have the ability to cope with them. No value should be placed here! When you suppress your emotions, you negate one natural response to the events.

Employees are frequently cheated of both the joy and frustration of top management's reactions to a project's progress. Business may be measured by the bottom line, but people express emotions in response to both success and failure.

Anger. The fourth element of emotional reflexology deals with perception of anger. Anger, when vented at lower stages of conflict, can bring about a catharsis, helping the parties identify issues and values involved. Anger expressed during higher stages of conflict has the opposite effect. Emotional reflexology causes us to employ anger inappropriately, using anger at higher stages and avoiding it at lower stages, exactly the opposite of its proper use.

The inappropriate use of anger may stem from rising frustration over a conflict and cause an explosion of emotions resulting in unwanted words and misplaced blame. Others have an inordinate desire to "look in control" and suppress their anger early in a conflict. In both cases, at lower stages of conflict emotional reflexology causes us to squelch anger, assuming it will pass.

During higher stages of conflict, we finally exceed our toleration level and express the anger, usually inappropriately. Once higher stages of conflict are reached, it is obvious that everyone is angry and the anger serves little value. One excellent management technique for handling anger in the higher stages of conflict is to say: "It is clear that everyone is angry, but it will help us little to escalate our emotions. I recognize your anger and will seriously consider your concerns. There is no longer a need to vent those emotions in this setting."

The proper focus of anger is at issues, not at people. That is hard to remember once the people and problem are intertwined. Along with anger is the threat of danger to other parties. If anger is expressed at stage three, it can be dangerous since the goal of each side is to get rid of the other party.

Five Emotional Don'ts During Conflict

1. **Don't Get in a Power Struggle.** There is a significant relationship between power and authority. Most sociologists acknowledge the fact that as power increases, authority decreases and vice versa. Well known sociologist Erik Erikson noted that children become emotionally disturbed when they possess power they cannot responsibly handle. Psychologist Emile Durkheim discovered that clearly defined norms and rules are needed to govern life, or people become self-destructive.

   One creative response you can bring to conflict is an ability to give away power, allowing others to take control of their feelings and the event in question.

   Your authority increases when you empower others instead of getting into power struggles. Power tends to be coercive; authority involves a sense of respect. If you can find a way to turn aside power struggles, you'll be more effective during conflict.

   Try these ideas:

   • Don't argue unless you are prepared to waste time. Reason won't work.

- Don't engage in a battle unless you are prepared to lose because you already have.

- Don't take total responsibility for others' emotions. Share the responsibility.

2. **Don't Detach From the Conflict.** At first, this may seem contradictory, but it is actually a way to monitor conflict and keep it under control. It is important that you have a passionate concern for both the people and the problem. Business will not operate without people, and it cannot operate efficiently until substantive conflict is managed. Concern is one motivation that drives us to find the opportunity in conflict.

3. **Don't Let Conflict Establish Your Agenda.** Time management specialists suggest it is imperative to do the truly important tasks, not the urgent. This principle is often distorted under the pressure of conflict, and many important business matters are ignored in an attempt to deal with the conflict.

Perspective is the key. In conflict, the individual must know both the goals and direction in which to move. Decision and responses to conflict should match this overall direction. But sometimes urgent needs interfere with daily schedules. A time study should reveal that you have spent time managing priorities and not managing conflict unendingly.

Here are some tips to help you manage the urgent:

a. Don't spend all your time and energy on one issue.

b. Watch time traps. Are there tasks that always seem to consume your time before you're aware it's gone?

c. Identify urgent issues, especially negative or conflict issues. If you notice one consistent time offender, manage that offender.

   — Are co-workers delegating to you and getting you to do their work?

   — Do they bring solutions or just concerns and requests?

   — Do they feed your moan-and-groan needs? It's easy to get caught in a negative cycle, and there are always people and events that can feed a poor-me syndrome.

4. **Don't "Awfulize."** Joan Borysenko, author of *Minding the Body, Mending the Mind*, defines awfulizing as "the tendency to escalate a situation into its worst possible conclusion." The intensity of the conflict determines which strategies will be the most effective. It is easy to be pushed to worst-case scenarios when faced with stage two or three conflict. Those locked into higher levels of conflict lose their ability to quantify the intensity of the problem.

Reminders to avoid awfulizing:

• People are rarely as benevolent as they perceive themselves to be.

85

- People are rarely as evil as their opponents perceive them to be.

- Individuals rarely spend as much time thinking about the issues as believed by their opponents.

- The motivations of others are rarely as planned or thought out as presented. Most aspects of conflict spin off other events and are not the result of cold-hearted calculation.

- Every conflict has a history. The people and their previous patterns of relating taint the present perception.

5. **Don't be Fooled by Projection.** Projection is an emotional release. Individuals unconsciously project their own flaws and weaknesses onto others. To be effective during conflict, you should notice the generalizations and accusations being made about others, especially comments about someone's motivations. We may understand others and we may be able to predict their actions accurately, but it is dangerous to believe anyone can read the mind of others.

Growth or Loss?

Because conflict is rooted in emotion, it has potential for good or harm. It offers an opportunity for either growth or loss. When you handle conflict effectively, there are three areas of growth:

- **Your Personality.** Experiencing success in dealing with conflict builds your self-confidence, which in turn builds your self-esteem. People with high self-esteem tend to have more positive personalities.

- **Your Power.** Personal power, or trust, is built between people when they overcome their fear of self-disclosure. When dealing successfully with conflict, you likely used self-disclosure, which built trust and power.

- **Your Perspective.** When you have a conflict with someone, it's usually because they have a different perception of reality. By working through this conflict successfully, you've widened your own perspective.

Unfortunately, there can also be negative consequences of conflict. Here are three potential areas of loss:

- **Momentum.** Conflict can be an obstacle that stops some people in their tracks.

- **Self-esteem.** Those with whom you are in conflict may try to make you feel guilty, inadequate or stupid. Remember: the only person who can ever allow you to be manipulated is you.

- **Relationships.** A sad but true occurrence is when friends and family, the very people with whom your lines of communication could and should be the clearest, are torn apart because of conflict.

Obviously, you have much at stake. The end result of conflict is up to you.

Select a recent, successfully concluded conflict in your life. After careful consideration, determine a level for your personality, power and perspective before the conflict using a scale of 1 - 10 (1 being the lowest, 10 the highest). Then, using the same scale, determine a level for your personality, power, and perspective after the conflict's successful conclusion.

Using the before and after levels you've established, create a bar chart for each of these three areas of growth that illustrates the extent of your growth produced by that conflict. Then write a brief description of how you have grown in each area.

If you believe that you experienced no growth from the conflict, think again. Reconsider the events very carefully. It is rare that you will walk away from a successfully resolved conflict without growth in at least one area.

Emotional Issues Checklist

Create a Safe Environment
Yes   No
1. Have you shared hope and optimism?
2. Did you communicate that this is manageable?
3. Is it clear that no one needs to be hurt?
4. Did you communicate a concern for everyone's success?
5. Have you established equality:
   Put-downs not allowed?
   No punishments will be made?
   All feelings are acceptable?

Reflections

Meet the Internal Needs of Others
Yes   No
1. Did you communicate, "I care about you?"
2. Did you communicate, "I care about our relationship?"
3. Did you communicate, "I care about this company?"
4. Did you communicate, "I want you to have some input in how this will be resolved?"

Join the Issue ... Invite ... Confront
Yes   No
1. "We (not you) have a problem."
2. "Let's get started together."
3. Have you listened?
   Do you know as much about the other party as your own position?
   What are the facts?
   What are the feelings?
4. Have you separated fact from opinion?
5. Are you assuming or do you know?
6. What are the vested interests?
7. Are there multiple solutions?

Reflections

Reflections

Negotiation and mediation are used during the higher stages of conflict. Usually a negotiation or mediation team comes from outside the conflicting groups. Although the intervention team does not necessarily need to be from outside the company, it must be perceived by both parties as authoritative and capable of dealing fairly with all the issues. When you have completed this chapter, you'll know the five-step intervention process, how to select an intervention team, and how the team should operate.

Selecting the Intervention Team

An effective intervention strategy begins with a humble awareness that super-human skills are inadequate without the cooperation of others. Teamwork is essential to conflict management. All parties should have a part in the selection process following this procedure:

1. Determine how many people you need/want on your intervention team.

2. Create a list of potential team members. Include at least three times as many names as will be needed on the team.

3. Provide the conflicting parties with resumes for each individual.

4. Conduct a meeting with representatives from each side. Alternating between parties, each group will be allowed to delete one name from the list. This process will continue until only the predetermined number is left.

5. Those names that remain at the end of this process will form the intervention team.

8 THE INTERVENTION TEAM

Negotiation and mediation are used during the higher stages of conflict. Usually a negotiation or mediation team comes from outside the conflicting groups. Although the intervention team does not necessarily need to be from outside the company, it must be perceived by both parties as authoritative and capable of dealing fairly with all the issues. When you have completed this chapter, you'll know the five-step intervention process, how to select an intervention team, and how the team should operate.

Selecting the Intervention Team

An effective intervention strategy begins with a humble awareness that super-human skills are inadequate without the cooperation of others. Teamwork is essential to conflict management. All parties should have a part in the selection process following this procedure:

1. Determine how many people you need/want on your intervention team.

2. Create a list of potential team members. Include at least three times as many names as will be needed on the team.

3. Provide the conflicting parties with resumes for each individual.

4. Conduct a meeting with representatives from each side. Alternating between parties, each group will be allowed to delete one name from the list. This process will continue until only the predetermined number is left.

5. Those names that remain at the end of this process will form the intervention team.

The presence of an intervention team is evidence that things have escalated beyond the workable stage. Events must be controlled by an external source. The following guidelines can be helpful in establishing the intervention team.

Guidelines for an Intervention Team

Limit Hostility. There is little need for hostility once the intervention team is selected. The team's presence is an indication that lines are severely drawn. A deliberate de-escalation of hostility by the intervention team can be helpful in moving the conflict to more manageable levels.

Become Involved. The intervention team is capable of providing insight and creative alternatives. Once stage three conflict has been reached, resolution is mandatory. While lower-level conflict requires participation in the final outcome, ownership in a negotiated or mediated settlement comes with the exit of the intervention team.

Get a Note-Taker. An accurate record of conversations and events is critical to the team's ability to function effectively. The intervention team should secure an accurate note-taker rather than being required to divide their attention between substance and documentation.

The attention necessary to record the details can distract from efforts to resolve the conflict.

Brevity in Explanations. The intervention team will provide feedback during the process. This is a time for clear and factual reporting, not for speeches or lengthy explanations.

Shun Confidentiality. The intervention team will not deliberately violate individual positions, but the process of data gathering is extensive. The need to maintain confidentiality can inhibit the effectiveness of the intervention team. There is also a tendency on the part of the conflicting parties to tone down threats and accusations when confidentiality is not guaranteed, de-escalating the volatility of a stage three conflict.

Avoid Being a Rescuer. The intervention team offers only an external third-party perspective. It is easy to promise more than can be delivered. People want to make the intervention team responsible for solving problems and rescuing the group. Expectations run high once an intervention team has been identified, placing undue pressure on the team, often without a corresponding amount of pressure on the disputing parties. The responsibility for resolving the conflict remains with the disputing parties.

Begin an Accountability Process. Once an agreement has been reached through intervention, follow-up will be necessary to encourage and monitor compliance. An early focus on accountability can make the follow-up process easier.

Statements about issues or people must be accurate. Stage three conflict greatly exaggerates differences in perspective. The intervention team must be willing to confront categorical positions and ask if an individual is willing to be quoted on a point.

Deal with Rumors or Accusations Directly. During high intensity conflict, a delineation between people and problem is essential. Rumors abound during higher stages of conflict. One technique an intervention team can employ is to generate face-to-face dialogue. The following steps help control unsubstantiated statements.

- Ask if an individual is willing to go with you and discuss the issues face to face.

- If he refuses, ask if you can use his name and approach the other party with the facts expressed.

- If he again refuses, tell him emphatically that this issue will not be addressed further until he is willing to participate in its resolution and that no further discussion of these facts will be allowed.

The Five-Step Intervention Process

This five-step process is a suggested format for conducting a third-party intervention. An effective intervention team can serve as a catalyst to action and resolution even at the highest conflict stages but the success or failure of this format resides with the parties involved.

Step 1: Establish the ground rules

Step 2: Collect the data

Step 3: Frame the issues

Step 4: Generate alternatives

Step 5: Obtain agreement and spread the news

Step 1: Establish the Ground Rules. The intervention team must define standard operating procedures. Establishing firm ground rules builds credibility for the team and can set a positive tone.

- Everyone will be asked to speak in personal terms, using "I" statements rather than blaming or attacking others. The goal of the intervention team is not to affix blame but to find a solution.

- Assumptions will be met with skepticism. The intervention team is looking for verifiable facts. Once statements are made, the team will seek out the truth to confirm or deny the statement.

- The team will not become a filter for information that cannot be shared or verified. Confidentiality leads to insider information that is counter-productive to resolution.

- The intervention team is here to act as a catalyst for resolution. Problems must be solved by those involved; however, the intervention team provides an outside perspective that can be helpful.

- The presence of an intervention team indicates that serious problems exist. Calm and reason must prevail. Threats are unacceptable. Excessive hostility undermines resolution.

- The intervention team will conduct interviews, distribute questionnaires, and hold public information meetings as needed. Everyone will be kept informed. Conflicting parties will be asked to refrain from comments until the team has completed its findings.

Step 2: Collect the Data. The intervention team must gather information quickly. The conflicting parties should be able to provide a list of initial contacts that would be helpful. Information to be collected includes:

- A history of the conflict

- Communication patterns

- A distribution of perceived power

- The priority of the problem

The intervention team has two avenues for collecting the necessary information: questionnaires and personal interviews. While questionnaires may provide a way to get at data quickly, they have several drawbacks. They provide no opportunity for two-way communication, for seeking clarification to a point made, or to help separate fact from opinion. Questionnaires also fail to present all the subtleties of verbal communication, such as tone of voice or inflection. that reflect attitude and level of emotional involvement of the parties. Therefore, the preferable method for data collection is typically personal interviews.

Fairness, empathy, openness, and a sincere sense of objectivity should characterize the interview. The interviewer should provide non-verbal support to help the parties reduce anxiety and move toward an acceptance of the events. Listening techniques are of utmost importance.

Step 3: Frame and Reframe the Issues. Conflict listening is a specific listening skill that provides support to the speaker while clarifying feeling and issues. The chart illustrates conflict listening as a two-step process.

Conflict Listening

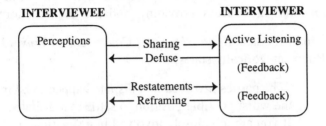

The first step (defuse) an interviewer must take is to hear everything an individual brings to the conflict. Many emotions, some extremely heightened, must be sifted through. Once these emotions have been identified, the interviewer speaks back to the party toning down (defusing) the emotions and separating the people from the problem.

In the best situation, the defusing will be effective, cooler heads will prevail, and the process can move forward. There is no guarantee, however, that the interviewer can move toward reframing. In the worst case, the party either will not desire or be able to separate people from problem. Others will de-escalate once they have been heard. The interviewer then identifies an impasse or defuses the situation.

Reframing involves a synthesis of issues and positions that accurately reflects an individual's perceptions, balanced by the interviewer's perspectives. Concessions can be identified for later use.

The interviewer is looking for the core issues, which will not be the same for everyone. Core issues, once collected, can be presented in a public meeting (framing), as part of the significant findings. The difference between reframing and framing is the arena. Reframing happens during individual or small group interviews. Framing takes place in a public meeting. During framing the intervention team enters the process, providing guidance and direction.

In his book *deBono's Thinking Course* author Edward deBono categorically states,

> "The parties involved in a dispute happen to be in the worst possible position to settle that dispute ... If you are too closely involved in a situation, it is difficult to get an overview or to get a sense of perspective."

The intervention team therefore brings the best available insight to a conflict. This process of intervention is not simply passive administration or a rehashing of the problems. The role of the intervention team is to design a solution that meets the needs of the group and encourages movement toward a positive use of the conflict.

The interview team frames the issues within a context of options. Conciliatory remarks can be suggested along with a wide range of alternatives. Framing is limited only by the creativity of the intervention team. The intention is to move the opposing parties toward more similar points of view.

Step 4: Generate Alternatives. A pilot was asked why cabin lights are dimmed prior to night landings. "We prepare for a worst-case scenario," he replied. "Since the landing presents the possibility of a crash, we want our passengers to be accustomed to the dark if the worst happens. Their eyes will be adjusted to the darkness so they can see to exit the plane."

Many people are shocked by worst-case scenarios. Yet the destructive nature of a stage three conflict can easily result in a worst case event. The direct presentation of a worst case situation is a valuable and dramatic illustration of the need for resolution. Sometimes the parties have to be face-to-face with the potential devastation of the worst case scenario to be willing to work together at all. Even then, some may dig in their heels and refuse to assist in the process.

Few stage three conflicts involve single issues. There are usually many points with varying degrees of disagreement and even occasional areas of agreement. The intervention team can move away from polarization while generating options by listing the points of convergence.

The intervention team must take charge by providing very specific leadership. Work with the easy issues first. This creates a cumulative effect that builds as parties spend time working together. The longer people remain in the process, the more they tend to be invested in an answer. Once the easy concessions have been defined, the core issues can be addressed.

Generating alternative solutions in a stage three conflict is painfully difficult. Parties do not trust each other or want to work together. The intervention team might pursue the generation of ideas:

- Require parties to argue the opposing position.

- Have individual participants complete these questions in writing anonymously.

    1. What is the minimum I can accept?

    2. What is the maximum I can go for without getting thrown out of the room?

    3. What is the maximum I can give away?

4. What is the least I can offer without getting thrown out of the room?

Use the answers or starting points for discussions.

• Relieve the tension with some type of humorous team exercise. (Expect great resistance.)

• Ask, how would a martian solve this problem? Attilla the Hun? Mother Teresa?

• The intervention team can present ideas of its own.

When a viable idea is introduced, the intervention team can poll the group and test an option. If it flies, the beginnings of a working solution can be formulated.

The core issues may still present problems. The intervention team must be open to all points. As convergence happens, some will feel they are looking into a tunnel that is getting narrower. This squeeze must reflect new directions and perspectives. A new group has formed and the group is headed into new territory together.

Once the ideas and best alternatives have been presented, the intervention team should call a break, move to a different room, and begin the process of sifting through the issues. The new setting should have a conciliatory atmosphere with a big picture perspective. The organization's mission statement and vision should be readily visible.

Seating should be circular rather than face to face. It is harder to polarize around a round table. Negative and reactionary feelings may arise, and the intervention team must be willing to stop all input with a quick comment. "That has been heard and we have attempted to deal with it. Please help us focus on the future now."

Last-resort options include voting on the alternatives and compromise. With voting, one side wins and the other loses. All parties must be informed before this strategy is implemented that they MUST comply if they lose. People tend to be more willing to compromise once the alternatives of all-win or all-lose have been presented.

Compromise is left as a last resort option because it reflects no winners. In a compromise solution there are almost winners and almost losers. The compromise is perceived as a tie. Once a conflict has reached stage three, ties usually are not satisfying for anyone, but they may be better than losing everything. If the process breaks down, a worst-case scenario may result.

Stage three conflict is polarized around personalities. Leaders and spokespeople are apparent, but the intervention team does not want to encourage conferences by these leaders of the various factions. Keep the solution contained within the group of representatives all agreed. It will be the role of the intervention team and the spokespeople to present the results to the parties.

Step 5: Obtain Agreement and Spread the News. A letter of consensus should be drafted by the head of the intervention team. This letter lists in a positive manner the conclusions that have been reached. This letter includes these three areas:

- We met ...

- We discussed ...

- We did ... or, we agreed ...

Although the decision has been hammered out by the parties and the intervention team, a sales job must follow. The rest of the company must be informed of the decision.

First, spokespersons from all perspectives must be seen together with a member of the intervention team. True ownership is communicated when all those involved in the decision stand together and explain the conclusions. DO NOT allow the spokespeople to speak privately to their own group. It is easy in a face-saving manner, to project a "this is the best we could do" attitude. The intervention team and spokespeople want to communicate a "this is a great alternative to our problem" stance.

The second point is to delineate when and where people may go to pursue the conclusion in private. The intervention team must be willing to enter into a defuse and reframe position with those most intensely involved. This requires a very firm hand on the part of the intervention team. This defuse and reframe time should be conducted in the presence of a member from all sides and led by a member of the intervention team.

The Along-Side Plan

Finally, the management staff that initiated the formation of an intervention team should have developed an along-side strategy for business over the past weeks that provides time to work with people across the barriers that have developed. Management must be creative in developing workable, positive interactions. The key to moving in a positive direction is an emphasis on the new team.

Here are some ideas for building an along-side plan:

- Identify individuals from both sides that are not affected by the conflict.

- Identify people who have the greatest investment in losing, and seek a buy-in from them to
work toward meaningful results.

- Find ways to generate meaningful teamwork
and work toward the completion of short-term
company, department or division goals.

- Disputants that are entrenched in stage three
should be identified and given short-term, easy-
to-complete tasks. This builds confidence and
provides opportunity to suggest that until the
conflict is settled favorable for everyone, the
risk of extensive involvement in team projects
and goals would be unwise.

- Establish a big picture focus that clearly identifies to all parties that the company is larger
than the conflict. Foster an attitude that things
will continue and that people are expected to
work with one another.

Even those not in sales must deal with customers every
day. A customer is anyone inside or outside your organization who utilizes or benefits from your services. Meeting
all those diverse needs is an extremely important and virtually impossible task.

Anger is a frequent response to unmet needs or expectations. Whether a customer's anger is justified in any given
situation is really irrelevant. It is a reality and must be dealt
with as quickly and efficiently as possible. When you've
completed this chapter, you'll have ten conflict management tools specifically for dealing with angry customers.

Consider a conflict within your organization. Could an intervention team be helpful?

- Who can you put on the team? If you're not in a position to put together a team, identify the people you'd appoint if it were your decision to make.

- When will you begin putting the team together? When will you approach your boss with the idea of an intervention team and with your suggestions for who might serve on it?

Reread this chapter changing every reference to company to read family.

- How would you go about putting together an intervention team to deal with those volatile personal issues?

- Who could be objective while serving on the team?

- When will you ask them to serve?

Reflections

9 DEALING WITH ANGRY CUSTOMERS

Even those not in sales must deal with customers every day. A customer is anyone inside or outside your organization who utilizes or benefits from your services. Meeting all those diverse needs is an extremely important and virtually impossible task.

Anger is a frequent response to unmet needs or expectations. Whether a customer's anger is justified in any given situation is really irrelevant. It is a reality and must be dealt with as quickly and efficiently as possible. When you've completed this chapter, you'll have ten conflict management tools specifically for dealing with angry customers.

Ten Tips for Soothing Angry Customers

1. **It's not personal.** By being on the front line, you are the punching bag to absorb the customer's frustrations about problems and conflicts. It's not you; it's the situation.

2. **Keep your cool.** Returning the customer's anger with like responses will only escalate the situation even further. Keep yourself under control: cool, calm, not angry, not defensive.

3. **Defuse the anger.** Let the customer get it all off his chest. He needs to vent. Eventually, he

will run out of steam. Until he does, however, nothing you can say will have any impact on him. Because of his highly emotional state, the logic of your responses or explanations will simply not register with him and may even make him more volatile. Wait him out.

4. **Be sympathetic.** The customer not only wants you to understand the problem, he wants you to understand his reaction to it. Right now, this situation is the most important thing on his mind and indifference or defensiveness on your part will further alienate him.

5. **Listen attentively.** Let the customer finish. Ask questions to clarify what the customer is saying.

6. **Don't make promises you can't keep.** It is all too easy to jump in and make a hasty promise to appease a hostile customer. Don't do it. It will only cause more problems down the road.

7. **Analyze the problem.** Angry customers are typically so intent on making sure you understand their anger that they fail to express the real problem clearly. It is up to you to uncover the underlying problem. Ask open-ended, probing questions and repeat what the customer has said to ensure your full understanding.

8. **Ask the customer exactly how he would like the problem resolved.** If it is within your power to comply, do so. If not, negotiate a satisfactory solution.

9. **Emphasize what you can do.** "Let me see what I can do for you," will help defuse the customer's ire while, "I don't know what we can do about it" will inflame him. Avoid the helpless, "I only work here" or "it's against company policy." This infuriates people. Even if it is against company policy, find a different way to tell the customer that you cannot do what he is requesting.

10. **Act on the problem and follow through.** Once you've told the customer what will be done, do it. If parts of it are to be done by other departments, follow up with them to ensure the necessary actions were taken. Otherwise, you'll have the pleasure of dealing with this hostile customer in yet another volatile situation.

- Outline a recent conflict with an angry or hostile customer.

- How well did you handle it? What exactly did you do?

- How would you handle the situation differently in the future?

- Rank the 10 tips by how good you are at them already (10 being the best and 1 being your weakest area). Focus on one tip per week until you've developed proficiency in all of them.

Reflections

10 A PARTING PHILOSOPHY

Everything can be taken from a man but one thing: the last of the human freedoms – to chose one's attitude in any given set of circumstances, to choose one's own way."

–Victor Frankl

We may not be able to avoid all conflict. We may not be able to resolve everything the way we'd like. We may find many things beyond our control. But we CAN control the approach and the mindset we take into every situation.

Follow this Six-Step Model when dealing with conflict and confrontation:

1. Listen
2. Acknowledge
3. Explain
4. Seek alternatives
5. Use assertive statements
6. Summarize the discussion

Because the pace of life is so rapid, many of us live with great intensity. That intensity may propel us forward in a competitive business environment, but a more reserved, contemplative approach might be more effective in our pursuit of conflict management.

Points to Ponder

- Accept life as it is ... conflict and all.

- Accept yourself and be true to your own values and beliefs.

- Accept others as they are, even all their short-comings and annoying habits.

- Be willing to clearly, calmly and gently let your needs, wishes, and position be known.

- Allow others to express their needs/wishes/position without interruption.

- Look for common ground, areas of agreement and mutual concerns.

- Recognize that although a particular issue may seem critical at the time, in the overall scheme of life it just may not be that monumental after all.

- Differences should be recognized, respected, and utilized rather than rejected and resented.

- Reduce fear in others by legitimizing their right to be heard and by receiving their point of view as valid.

- Practice the art of active and listening.

- Learn to let the initial wave of emotion pass without imputing grave consequences to the occasion.

- Understand that feelings are not bad; only destructive behavior is bad.

- Say something good about another person or event before saying what you don't like.

- Being aware of how people react to words and actions and understanding the emotional climate of a group are two examples of the insights that are helpful to successful conflict resolution.

- A calm, reasoned response is always better than a hasty reaction.

SUGGESTED READING

"Response-Ability — the ability to choose your own response. What matters most is how we respond to what we experience in life."

Stephen Covey

Anderson, Kare. *Getting What You Want: How to Reach Agreement and Resolve Conflict Every Time*

Borisoff, Deborah and David A. Victor. *Conflict Management: A Communications Approach*

Bramson, Robert. *Coping with Difficult Bosses*

Bramson, Robert. *Coping with Difficult People*

Carr-Rufino, Norma. *Managing Diversity: Skill Builder*

deBono, Edward. *deBono's Thinking Course*

Fisher, Robert and William Ury. *Getting to Yes: Negotiating Agreement Without Giving In*

Hendrie, Weisenger, Ph.D. *Anger at Work: Learning the Art of Anger Management on the Job*

Levine, Stewart. *Getting to Resolution, Turning Conflict into Collaboration*

Ury, William. *Getting Past No: Negotiating Your Way from Confrontation to Cooperation*

INDEX

A
Acceptance 52-53, 76-79, 96
Aggression 49, 59-60
Anger 4-6, 13-14, 22-23, 45, 49, 60-61, 78-83, 105-107, 113
Anxiety 56, 76-77, 95-96
Arbitration 28-30
Auditory 64
Avoiding 35, 38-39, 48, 82

B
Blaming 80-81, 94-95
Borysenko, Joan 85
Bridges, Robert 77
Broken record technique 69, 71

C
Collaborating 35, 36
Compromising 40-41, 48
Conflict management style 35-36, 38-41, 44-48
Constructive Confrontation Model 67-69, 71
Cooperate 1, 15, 18, 33-34, 50, 55, 69, 80-81, 91, 113
Coping 12-13, 21-26, 31-32, 39-40, 56, 65, 80-81, 91
Covey, Stephen 113

O

Obliging 23-24, 26, 35-37, 48, 56-57, 65

P

Passive style, 56-58
Power struggle 83

R

Rejection response 76, 78-79
Repressed feelings 80, 81-82
Retaliate 14, 18

S

Secrecy 3, 80, 81
Stage one conflict 22-25, 65, 79-80
Stage three conflict 22, 27-30, 92-94, 98-101
Stage two conflict 25-27, 41, 53, 65
Stress 5-6, 11-12, 18-20, 64, 74-75, 78-79

V

Visual 64